SIMULATED HYSTERIA

Simulated Hysteria

Trent Portigal

MANDELSTUCK EDITIONS

705, 10303 111 STREET

EDMONTON

First Printing, 2020

ISBN 978-1-7772650-0-7

Design: Rio Saxon Design

SACRIFICES

The notebook has two faces. One for sacrifices, the other for sins. Writing that here, in the notebook, feels weird. It's on the cover. If you're reading this, you already know what's on the cover. I guess you might be wondering why I'm writing on the sacrifices side. Is this a sacrifice? Writing? No. I don't think so. Reading my writing might be. An escape? An inward-looking escape, all self-absorbed, if it is. Not getting lost in fantasy, denial, anything like that. Just spending some time with myself, to better understand myself, my condition. Let's go with that. What is clear: writing is not a symptom of my condition. I'm writing on the sacrifices side because that was the side up, when Nurse Galverson gave it to me. Don't know if she thought it through. Like, she didn't want me to immediately think I'm sinful, that there's something wrong with me. She knows something's wrong. It's why I'm here. That's not the question. More like she wanted to avoid conflict, unnecessary conflict. I would turn to the sins side when I was ready, when I chose, as needed. Or something like that. More likely only if I run out of room. I'm just writing on the side I started on, the side already facing me. In the writing room of a hospital, where I'm a client. It would be weird to sit in a writing room not writing. So, I am writing.

I wasn't writing, though. I didn't have anything to write on. Until Nurse Galverson gave me this notebook. Maybe she thought it was weird I was sitting here, in the writing room, not writing. Staring at the wall, sort of through the wall. It's kind of a blue-grey colour, like a foggy day. It's just mist, nothing but vapour. You're sure you can sort of see something through it, but maybe your mind is playing tricks on you. My mind doesn't play tricks on me, to be clear. I don't believe I can see through the wall, I know the wall's solid. The colour isn't hard, is all. The doctors probably chose it because of that. Hard edges lead to conflict. They wanted to avoid conflict, just like Nurse Galverson. I was looking at the wall, balanced awkwardly on a hard wooden chair at the central table. Don't know why I described the chair as hard right then. Most of the chairs here are metal. The wood is soft, in comparison. It just feels hard, I guess because I am so much softer, don't really fit its form, all right angles. The room reeked of varnish. It still smells. The table had been recently stripped, sanded, refinished. For a while, the writing room just had a couple of desks, for children or small people. All that effort, the stripping, sanding, refinishing, to erase the thoughts scratched, cut into the surface. Traces remain, though can't make out the meanings. Might never have had much meaning, much thought. Not a lot of coherence around here, at the hospital, among the clients. I am a client. Used to be an inmate. Then a patient. Now a client. There were kids here, when I was an inmate, but they're gone now. They probably got new desks, wherever they are now. There's still hope for kids, that they'll get better, so they get money. I guess redoing the table must have cost something. Not much, that sort of work is done by other clients, in the shop, for skills training. Life skills are important. Even then, probably something gouged into the wood was hurtful, would have led to conflict. Forced the head doctor's hand. I didn't pay attention. Conflict's not something I seek out. If you're reading this, you're probably thinking I had a surface to write on all along, right in front of me, except when it was in the shop. I was too busy looking at the wall, lacking the imagination to see through it, I guess, beyond the institution, and to see my writing as sculpture. It's not as if I would be hurting the table. The wood is dead. I just know it would have been wrong to do that. The table is not mine to mark. I know right from wrong. Sometimes the difference seems like mist, barely there, but it is there, like the wall.

The notebook was given to me, to write in. Nurse Galverson said so. She even put my name on it, on the sacrifices side. I guess it was a leftover she had, lying around. Like something given to kids in fancy Catholic schools, where sin and sacrifice still have meaning. A guide to life. A clear and proper ledger. Not too many clients come from that background, but there are a few. A strange object, to find here, but no odder than not writing in the writing room. And buying a new notebook would have been unthinkable. Sometimes I feel like a kid, but I know that's no longer true. I can last on the outside, I can manage my condition. I can't get better.

I guess I should start, with my name. I feel like a Jacquot. That's what they called me, at the archives. I worked at the National Archives for a while, digitizing records. It was good. The doctors always try to steer us to some sort of institution, when we leave the hospital. A stable, routine environment. Medical institutions, hospitals, where they can handle a relapse, are preferred. Hospitals only need so many orderlies and janitors, though. Some of the staff here are former clients. For me, that time, the institution was the National Archives.

I can write pretty well, when I have something to write on. Not all clients can write well. Not that I wrote anything at the archives. I just scanned things. I guess the scanner scanned things. I put those things in the scanner. I was put in the animals group. We were in charge of the records for the National Zoological Park. Just a fancy way to say a zoo. So I put in lists of animals the zoo had. Lists of food they ate. Lists of diseases and conditions. Monkeys got ornery when they got old. Cats lost the use of their legs. And then there were whole books, each containing an expedition to Asia, Africa, South America. Animals bought, animals hunted, animals donated. Some didn't last a day in captivity. Some made it to the zoo and lived there for decades. Stable, routine environments aren't for everyone.

I was born into it. Lots of animals were born in the zoo, but later. At the beginning, if they came from captivity, it was from circuses. Animals with conditions that no longer drew crowds, repulsed people even. Sometimes it was just their ordinary way of being, incompatible with life on a stage, in a ring, in a cage. Sometimes it was a disease, usually ordinary in its own way, just not exactly a part of them. Not innate. Sometimes curable, sometimes marking the end, gradual or sudden. At the archives, I was an exotic animal, but not magnificent or beautiful. Not a freak or an alien either. Just different, weird. It was hard to tell whether it was me or the knowledge that I had come from captivity, that I had a condition, that made people see me like that. Hard to differentiate the one from the other. I guess I neither draw crowds nor repulse people. I just walk around with a little circus ring around me. I catch people looking at me like an audience watching a performance. A gap, uncrossable, inevitable, between us.

That takes me away from the zoo. Back in the days of inmates, this would have been a zoo. A lifetime locked away, no expectation to perform, except in the most basic way. Feeding, defecating. No efforts to manage the condition. No chance to leave, not really. Outside the hospital, I come across people who think it weird I am there, outside, in the world, interacting with them and everything they consider ordinary. I am not a lion, a tiger or a bear. There is a fear, exhilaration in the circus, that the animal so calm, doing tricks, could break away, revert to their wild state, harm themselves and others. Outside the circus, the exhilaration is swapped, for a feeling somewhere between unease and dread. Distance is maintained. People are impressed I can calmly feed documents into a scanner, day after day. Pages upon pages of daily records of animals in the zoo, feeding, defecating. There's always risk of an incident. People angry I was ever let out of my cage, the no risk is an acceptable risk folks, are rare. And I'm good at managing my condition. Back to the zoo, then. Or wherever here is. I am here, surrounded by blue-grey walls, writing in a non-sacrificial sort of way. When I was in the world, I had to perform, manage all the time. Nothing was natural. I learn a lot of skills here, but not how to be normal. I was anxious all the time. I was exhausted all the time. Feeding documents into the scanner was only the first step. The next was optical character recognition. The computer tried to make sense of the lines, the curves, the dots and always did a pretty good job. A pretty good job that was never good enough. I had to go through and correct the errors, wiping away any trace that the machine couldn't really read the words, understand the ideas. I felt closer to the machine than to the people around me. I envied it. I wished I had someone there to correct my interpretation errors, to break me out of my ring, close the distance between me and these animals that seemed so like me, yet so incomprehensible.

Jacquot is a generic name for a parrot. Lucien started calling me that the hundredth time I didn't react properly to something said. Digitizing records was apparently boring, tedious work. Everyone around me thought so. They filled the air with stories, banter that bounced around randomly from topic to topic. It wasn't random, I guess, not really. I just couldn't keep up, process it. It seemed random, to me. I liked the rhythm of scanning, recognizing, correcting. The words corrected I understood, mostly. What I didn't understand was normal to not understand. Technical, biological terms. Even those, I got a hang of a lot of them, if the animal lived long enough. The zoo's first struthio molybdophanes lasted 24 years. Repetition in context, why I ended up in the archives in the first place. At the hospital, they teach clients that we need to interact, with others, to fit in outside the walls. I couldn't just say nothing, concentrate on scanning, recognizing, correcting. To be safe, I repeated. I tried to learn the tricks to perform in my little ring, for my audience. But the context was constantly shifting. I ended up sounding like a parrot, a generic parrot named Jacquot. Pronounced Jack-o. As in Jack-o-lantern. With a shaky, sputtering flame the only activity between his ears. Alone in the writing room, with the emptiness of the room around me, I have a steady flame. Without effort, I burn slowly, evenly, and my brightness suites the space. At the end of a day, at the archives, I felt like I had sputtered out, like there was nothing left. If only I was a parrot.

I corrected observations on the great apes, including N'Gi the gorilla. I noticed regular comparisons to the development of people. N'Gi playing like a six-month old might, responding to visitors' waves like an eighteen-month old and so on. Following these observations was always an asterisk, with a note that the comparisons had no scientific bases. They were loose analogies, attempts to make the behaviours more relatable, not to be taken seriously. Apes just seemed so human-like. Maybe that's changed. We were digitizing old records. I know Lucien started calling me Jacquot as a loose comparison, a light-hearted observation, nothing more. I guess it was hard to tell at the beginning. Over time, it became clear. For a while, it made my life easier. It was good enough for me to be human-like, even if that was at odds with what clients were taught, in the hospital. We are fully human. Period. Human-like meant less effort, less anxiety. Until the name escaped our little room into the rest of the building, full of raw concrete blocks with sharp edges. Strangers, to me at least, took it to mean less-than-human. I never felt so isolated in my little ring, an unassuming little bird in the middle of an audience impatient to hear the miracle of speech.

I am alone in the writing room, writing now I have something to write on. No one writes in the writing room anymore. They write in the computer room. Cameras were installed, in the writing room, to make it easy to see who was left. I still feel alone. The official name of the computer room is Life Skills Laboratory, which I guess is only somewhat misleading, being only one of the many places clients learn life skills. In that room, clients write to learn how to write and to connect to others beyond the walls. The hospital is some distance from the city. Lots of people here find it isolated. The head doctor, Doctor Wimsatt, has said more than once she finds it terribly dull, so far from the madding crowd. Then she looks away and makes a noise halfway between a snort and a laugh. When she looks back, her face is blank, but a blank the furthest thing in the world from the blank concrete of the archives. With the wooded grounds in the walls and vast fields outside them, where farmers grow all manner of crops, I think this is a very busy place. I wonder if the animals in the zoo wouldn't be happier, wandering the grounds here. I write in the writing room because I have no family, friends to write to or hear from. It's for the best. Family and friends are either too poor to drive all the way out here, for a visit, or too rich to take the trip, risk being associated with the human-like. Certain things have not changed much since we were inmates. Why can't we just get better?

Human-like mammals were brought, to the zoo, from faraway lands. Long expeditions were mounted, vast sums of money spent, political favours traded. They were prized. So long as they looked healthy, they didn't even need to perform. Being there, alive, feeding, defecating, was enough. It seems simple, but lots of animals refused to eat and died. If a client refuses to eat for long enough, the doctors immobilize him, stick him with a feeding tube or IV needle. He isn't prized, sought out. But human life must continue. At the zoo, they experimented with different foods, different amounts for the human-like and other exotic life. If nothing worked, they concluded the animal didn't do well in captivity. But they already know humans can live a long time, locked away. They know what to feed them. If nothing works, the doctors conclude it is a symptom of the client's condition. Self-harm. I guess I wish they weren't so sure of what we needed to eat to survive. Then maybe they'd be willing to spend more money on it.

N'Gi the gorilla was special. Most observations were in the plural. The wolves did something, the beavers did something else, the seals, the otters and so on. If one escaped, it got some individual attention. It was still not enough for a name. A name required personality, interaction. N'Gi wore a double boiler, as a hat, and stood on his head from time to time. He would play with balloons, newspapers, balls. Whatever he did was normal, for him. It was also popular. He didn't have to perform. Chac the chacma baboon didn't perform much, got a sort of name. Chac the union monkey, they called him. At 4:30, his workday was over. He retired to his little house, closed the door. Another loose analogy, something relatable. An aspect of the daily grind of the masses as amusing character trait. I guess a lot of people in the audience did that sort of work, tedious labour. Or maybe the audience was full of people who thought the people who did that sort of work were human-like. Don't know. All the records scanned were on the animals in the cages. Anyway, I find Jacquot fitting. It gives me a name without making me special. Even if some people still expect me to stand on my head, on a double boiler, which would be on my head. People outside, in the world. Not at the hospital. Not in the writing room, where I can write, and it's normal.

Doctor Wimsatt reads this notebook. Everything clients write is read by the doctors or nurses, or both. Even emails written in the computer room. It is one way to find out how we are managing our conditions. If you are not Doctor Wimsatt and you are reading this, I meet with Doctor Wimsatt regularly. I meet with her in her office, in a small building off to the side, partially hidden by trees. She lives there, in that building. It looks like a cottage.

When we were inmates and children were at the hospital, they were told by older inmates the building was the cabin from Hansel and Gretel. A witch lived there who was going to fatten them up, eat them. They would be protected if they did things. I don't remember if I believed the story. I guess I never really understood it. I did things because I was small, afraid of everything. Then the reforms came. Children were separated, sent to another hospital. I was old enough to stay until I was prepared for the world. I was no longer an inmate, after all, and had some skills. My condition wasn't severe. I couldn't live in a cage forever.

Doctor Wimsatt is the first female head doctor. I haven't noticed a difference. Except that she keeps a bottle of gin in a drawer, in her desk. The last head doctor, Doctor Todd, kept bourbon, in the same place. Wimsatt pours some into her coffee cup after drinking the coffee, swirls it around to pick up the grounds left at the bottom. Todd poured his liquor into his coffee before drinking it. If I was to use a loose analogy without any scientific basis, they both seem like Soko the chimpanzee, when he got old and disillusioned, if the veterinarians would have allowed him to self-medicate. According to the records, he was melancholic, prone to erratic and violent outbursts. Luckily, the head doctors are doctors and know how to soften the edges, avoid conflict. It is still sad they seem to view the cottage at the edge of the woods like a cage they will never escape, especially when they try so hard to find us a place, in the world beyond the walls. They will be released, of course, when they retire. When their own body confines them. Women are rare at the hospital, yet their influence is always felt. If there were people in the blue-gray fog, they would be the mothers and sisters who send and get the lion's share of emails. They find a way to come for a visit, once or twice a year. They prepare the landing pad for clients judged ready to leave the hospital. With that support, maybe I would have lasted longer at the archives. Maybe

I wouldn't be in the writing room, writing, in this notebook. All the clients here are men. That's why women are rare. When I was an inmate, children and adults were mixed together. Women and men never were. I can't imagine Doctor Wimsatt as a mother or sister. A mother or sister living here, on hospital grounds, seems wrong somehow. I wonder what it's like at hospitals for women.

Lions, tigers and bears. The records show a lot of large predators donated to the zoo, by families that could no longer handle them. They got them when the animals were young, as pets. They were cute, I guess, playful. Then they grew up. A playful swipe was no longer playful. Keeping them fed became too expensive, too much of a burden. These families are considered normal. Sometimes I think not really understanding normal is a good thing. That's how I came to the hospital, as an inmate. My foster family wrote to the authorities, told them I was a burden. I was acting out, having episodes, incidents. Maybe it was epilepsy, some sort of seizures, they didn't know. It was just too much, I guess. I don't blame them, the family. The note was given to the institution. I was picked up, passed through Saint Anne's, sorted and sent here. It was my foster mother who wrote the message, sent it. The doctors and everyone else talked to her. I found out later my case wasn't unusual, except the foster part. Things changed since then. Clients are more like wild dogs now. Most come to the zoo through some sort of animal control. Either the Biological Survey or the Fish and Wildlife Service. If they were judged dangerous to people, inapt to life in the outside world, the service would offer them to the zoo. If a cage wasn't available, if they were too much even for the zoo, they were put down. Clients, being human, wouldn't be put down, to be clear. It's a loose analogy. A mother's note means less now, is all I want to say. At least as far as committing her kid.

Epilepsy, mental retardation.
Mental retardation with epilepsy.
Epilepsy, mental retardation.
Mental retardation with epilepsy.
Hysterical seizures.
Simulated hysteria.
Imbecility.
Epilepsy.
Retardation and instinctive perversions, epileptic-like attacks, physical signs of degeneration.
Mental retardation with intellectual confusion and morbid impulses.
False epileptic.
Mental retardation with instinctive perversion.
Mental degeneration, madness and poor instincts.
Severe Depression, hypochondriac.
Mental disability with epilepsy.

The above are all the diagnoses, for my father. Over twenty years of opinions. I have something to write in now, so I wrote them down. Doctor Wimsatt brought up my father, when we met. She had read the notebook. It was on her desk between us, beside my father's file. Doctor Todd also brought up my father. I'm sure he was used, at Saint Anne's, in deciding what to do with me. I knew about these opinions. I know both head doctors wonder about the reality of my condition. The doctors who examined my father wondered, too, about his condition. Only, no one knows who his father is. His mother died shortly after giving birth. She was poor, didn't have much use for doctors. There wasn't much to go on for family history. Now that I've worked in the archives, I don't think I do either. My father's file is full of guesswork, odd moral judgments. It's nothing like the meticulous records from the zoo.

Doctor Wimsatt wasn't interested, in the opinions. She handed me a bunch of slightly yellowed pages, covered with neat, careful writing, put together with a trombone. She slowly swirled the gin in the bottom of her coffee cup and observed me as I scanned the lines. Everything at the hospital is treated as a potential symptom. That's why I started writing by stating that writing is not a symptom. But denying this notebook is a symptom could be a symptom. It is up to the doctors to decide. The pages were my father's memoir, titled My Memoir. His mother died 13 days after giving birth. The only detail worth writing. The memoir was apparently addressed to the hospital director, the head doctor. A life story to convince the person who could let him out of his cage, that he didn't have a condition after all. It all started out as an act of a lonely orphan, placed in a store as an apprentice at a young age. Crises, attacks, episodes, incidents. All a confused attempt to get attention, avoid work, escape punishment. It worked, he kept doing it. Until the day the female half of the couple who ran the shop wrote a note, to the authorities. He was picked up, passed through Saint Anne's, sorted and sent wherever they had room for him. The doctors expected him to keep having attacks. They were his new audience. So he did. Until he knew better. By then it was too late. Unless the head doctor chose to let him out. Because he did know better. That was the argument. But he had known better before, before the memoir, had chances, to leave the walls, of the hospital, and failed. I guess the doctor wasn't convinced, by some words, neat and careful, on the page. My father died soon after, in the hospital.

Some animals can live just as well in captivity as in the wild. They can go back and forth. Beavers, elephants. Most can't. Once they are in the zoo, they never leave. There is no decision to make. Some escape. When beavers escape, they can make a nice go of it. Until a farmer kills them, as a pest. When an elephant escapes, it doesn't really escape. Not on this continent, anyway. My father was institutionalized. Maybe his condition was false or simulated. It didn't matter. Maybe, on some level, he understood, could manage his condition. He just couldn't adapt to the outside. I wrote before, that kids can get better. That's why money is spent on them. It isn't just that. They can adapt. Even in my father's time, the asylum, then hospital, wasn't supposed to be forever. It didn't help the supports weren't there, in the world, back then. Whatever the reasons, he always ended up on the street. Begged to come back. When he was back, he begged to leave. The memoir was a long plea. It was sad, frustrating. I am not my father, perhaps, but I'm not a child, beaver, elephant. I am here, in the hospital, writing. I had chances, support. Not a mother or sister, but I wasn't alone. Yet I am here.

Doctor Wimsatt asked me who I was writing for. I didn't know. She explained that that wasn't a bad thing. My father's memoir was coloured, she explained. He wanted to convince someone of something. It was better to just write, if I was going to spend so much time in the writing room. Not that I should be spending so much time in the writing room, alone, with the cameras. If I was, though. I didn't respond. I guess she took that as skepticism. She knew I knew that all writing was read. The notebook was in the middle of the desk. She had read it. That's why she showed me my father's memoir. Apparently, he spent a lot of time in the writing room, writing. Probably more than his memoir, though Doctor Wimsatt didn't show me any other yellowed sheets. They might not have been kept, in the file, if the doctors decided they weren't really a symptom, of his condition. He wasn't as alone. Computer rooms didn't really exist back then. Not in hospitals, for patients, before they were transformed, into clients. Doctor Wimsatt pulled open her gin drawer. She took out the bottle, put it between my father's file and the notebook. She said she wanted me to write about it. That she kept the bottle in her office, that she drank during the day. It was against the rules, contrary to professional ethics, she said. She would continue to read my writing, we would discuss it. She couldn't use it for an official diagnosis. That would get her fired, she'd lose her license. She called the gin a poison pill. Then she looked away and made a noise halfway between a snort and a laugh. Impulsive, self-destructive, just like Soko. Not really petty or selfish, though. Loose analogy, at best.

Chac the chacma baboon talked by smacking his lips. Observers couldn't agree on what Chac was saying, only that he was saying something. And that that something was reasonable and polite. He smacked his lips toward keepers and other humans he knew, who paid attention to him. When the brown hyenas moved in next door, Chac ignored them as best he could. Their mournful cries were apparently off-putting, the laughter unnerving. Keepers would hold the hyenas' food just outside the enclosure, until the animals started drooling and laughing. It amused the audience. Chac not so much, day after day, until 4:30, when he retreated into his little house, closed the door. The laughter was automatic. It was not like N'Gi standing on his head or Chac smacking his lips. The hyenas just did what they did. There was no changing it. Chac had no reason to get to know them better. Doctors frown on my spending so much time in the writing room, especially before I had something to write on. They would have preferred I interact more. To prepare me for the outside world. I wouldn't be in the hospital forever. Clients have more compulsions than a hyena. Tics, urges, manias. Without bars between Chac and the hyenas, there would have been conflict. In the outside world, baboons and hyenas wouldn't be so close together. In the writing room, I can avoid conflict. The blue-grey walls are solid enough to keep us apart. Doctor Wimsatt noted that I also don't write about people in the hospital. Not even Nurse Galverson, who was nice enough to give me this notebook, to write in. Maybe I'll write about her when I'm outside. Maybe I'm like my father, fixated on the outside when I'm inside and the inside when I'm outside. Even if the zoo is just another sort of inside.

Doctor Todd kept three skulls on his desk, along with pictures of bones tacked to a large cork board on the wall. Each skull was deformed, one too big for an ordinary brain, two too small. All three were small skulls, from children or small people. Each sat atop its own pile of paper. Doctor Todd joked that the pile under the big skull was all the big things he needed to deal with. The two other piles were small things. The piles of small things were always much larger than the pile of big things. Taken as a whole the small things were much bigger than the big things. He may not have been joking, it didn't seem like a real joke. Doctor Todd smiled a lot, but in a friendly, not funny, way. I remember wondering if he had eaten them, when I was small, the people the skulls belonged to. After hearing the Hansel and Gretel story. I didn't imagine the witch as a woman, just whoever lived in the cottage, partially hidden by trees. I stared at them, decided they were far too small to provide much for food. There were probably piles of skulls, other bones, hidden somewhere. Maybe in a basement, maybe buried on the grounds. His friendly smile seemed menacing, like a dog baring its teeth. In the zoo records, the word pickled was repeated regularly, as the last resort. If an animal didn't make it, it would be pickled and shipped off to the museum. The National Zoological Park was close to the National Museum. Some animals were pickled, in jars. Some stuffed and mounted. Sometimes the skin was peeled off for a pelt and the skeleton was put together with glue or screws. Expeditions to gather exotic life often brought it back both living and dead. Somewhere in the museum is probably a collection of human and human-like skulls. The museum keeps a little of everything. When I was young, I didn't think beyond the walls. Now I can, imagining whole continents of exotic animals through the blue-grey mist. But the blue-grey mist is a wall. I know I am inside. And I know people outside imagine clients, inside the walls, as somehow exotic. A generic Jacquot sort of exotic.

Doctor Todd took the skulls with him, or Doctor Wimsatt put them away somewhere. In either case, they disappeared when Doctor Todd retired. They were gone when I was back from the archives. Along with the tacked pictures. And the teeth. Doctor Wimsatt doesn't show her teeth, not in the same way, not baring them all in a friendly or threatening way. She seems less like a witch who eats children. I was too old by the time she became head doctor to believe in the story anyway. I'm not sure I ever really believed. I guess I never really understood it. I did things because I was small, afraid of everything. Then I got bigger, older, less afraid. All that seemed to happen at the same time. The fear didn't disappear, exactly. It just became anxiety, dread. I knew more. Not much, but more. I wouldn't be in the hospital forever. The keepers and attendants taught us things, prepared us for the outside. When we first met, Doctor Wimsatt had an article tacked on the cork board. As we met, regularly, other articles came and went, but that one stayed.

The Board and Garbage Bin Are Going to Die, the title. Marguerite Duras, the writer. It was there, in the background, as I read the neat lines, of my father's memoir. Two boys, men in the end, who grew up in care. Not in a hospital, making the story worse. The first named The Board because he was skinny. The second Garbage Bin because he ate anything and everything. They weren't going to be in care forever. There was money for boys, food, beds, life skills training. No computers. The article was dated 1958. They were released, at majority and didn't do well, outside, in the world. They got into a situation, got a couple of guns, held up some people, things went bad, two people died. The Board and Garbage Bin were caught, put on trial, sentenced to die. Don't think that can happen now, the death sentence. Human life has become more important, the government is no longer taking it, at least not like that. Not the point of the article. The Board and Garbage Bin couldn't understand the trial. They understood the basics, I guess. Nothing more. A priest was on trial at the same time, for killing two people. He understood the story, the sins and sacrifices of being human. How to perform, to connect, everything. He was not sentenced to die. He was seen as human, by the judge, the jury. The Board and Garbage Bin were not, needed to be put down. Human-like as less-than-human. I understood that at the archives, stuck in my ring. I understood it before, without knowing, I guess. When the fear went away, the anxiety took its place. The anxiety was a sort of understanding. The Board and Garbage Bin, in the accused box, their own ring, couldn't perform. They were taught skills, shoe-making, wood-working. But something else was needed, something was missing.

I'm in the writing room, writing. The blue-grey walls are soothing. The varnish is comforting, now that it isn't so strong. The kids who went to fancy Catholic schools, who would have gotten notebooks like this, also wrote. They knew to go back and forth between sacrifices and sins. To put their actions, thoughts in the right columns. And then talk about them, confess them, use the right words, with the priest. Not the same priest, the one that killed two people. Even if he too was part of the same world. Nurse Galverson gave me this notebook, to write in. I am writing in it. Here, in the writing room, in the hospital, maybe it doesn't matter what I write. Or maybe I'm on trial. Doctor Wimsatt reads the notebook. She'll decide whether I'm fit to leave these walls. If I have become too much like my father. I'm like N'Gi and the double boiler. I can use words, I can learn things. It can be amusing for the audience, on the other side of the bars. Using the boiler as a hat only strengthened the case that N'Gi wasn't human, that he couldn't leave. Letting

N'Gi out would have been a death sentence. I'm better than The Board and Garbage Bin. I amuse my audience, by repeating words, by being Jacquot. Dozens of journalists were at their trial, at the beginning. They weren't entertained, they didn't come back. The article tacked to the corkboard was the only one written, published about them. Maybe Nurse Galverson didn't know much about my time on the outside. Maybe she thought this notebook would help me be more human. Every word I write proves her wrong. All it shows is I know it's better to write in the writing room, when I have something to write on, than to gaze at the blue-grey wall. That's something, I guess.

I'm writing on a nightstand, in a hallway of the rooming house. Actually, I'm writing in the notebook, still on the sacrifices side. The notebook is on the nightstand. Everything is in the hallway. My room is empty. If you're reading this, you don't know I'm in a rooming house now, with a room to myself. My last words in the notebook were written where I was a client, in the hospital. I was turning into my father, or a zoo animal. I was never going to leave, not really. I couldn't last outside. My writing, in the writing room, was just begging the head doctor to be let out. Pretending I could manage my condition, maybe even that I didn't have a condition, that I had skills, that my thoughts connected together. Maybe they did, it was just not for me to decide. When exotic animals are bought or captured across the sea they are crated and shipped on enormous ships. The accounts show endless activity, cleverness. The size of the crate, what's in it, holes. Feeding, washing, defecating. Hippos had large pools built into their boxes. Elephants had holes in theirs large enough so their trunks could move freely outside them. Wine barrels replaced buckets to keep large animals watered. The details were endless. The transition from the wild to the zoo was the hardest part. Many didn't make it. If the seas were rough, most didn't make it. Animals were nervous, anxious, didn't eat for days. They were aware, but didn't understand. They saw a lot, but most was hidden. All but the elephants were kept in empty coal bunkers, protected from cold winds and fog. And some crates had bigger holes than others. That's how it felt when they decided I wasn't my father, at least not yet. Doctor Wimsatt, her bottle of gin, decided for the hospital. Someone I didn't know decided for wherever I was going. I mean, I met him. I just wasn't paying attention. Doctor Wimsatt says I don't pay enough attention, to people at the hospital, don't interact with them. The three of them decided. Then others prepared my transition. Once they knew where I was going, how I was likely to get there. I wrote, but in the computer room. The Life Skills Lab, because writing in the writing room was not a life skill. It didn't help me live, just become more like my father. Computer skills, cooking skills, money skills, everything was reviewed. The details were endless. And most were decided outside the coal bunker, like arranging a room in the rooming house. Since I didn't have a mother or sister.

I have an audience. In the hallway, people pass by. Unavoidable. The house has a common room, but people linger there. I'm not ready to linger with others, interact. Passing by is manageable. But a new neighbour is sitting on a chair, from my room. Now in the hallway. She's looking at me. Writing. In the writing room, there were two cameras. I was alone, but not alone. Easier to ignore cameras. Oksana. She said her name's Oksana. I said my name was Jacquot. I'm outside now. I have to interact, sometimes. At the hospital, they teach clients that we need to interact with others, to fit in outside the walls. Not something I seek out, but can't be rude. Being rude leads to conflict. She said Jacquot sounded like a nickname. I shrugged, continued writing. She is still there, perched on the chair, as I write. Maybe I should stop writing, say more. Maybe she should stop sitting on my chair, stop lingering, in the hallway. Clients in the hospital were always lingering, most places. But not in the writing room, where I wrote. Clients in the hospital thought of themselves as kings, presidents, philosophers. Some, anyway. They were special, important, at least to themselves. Before Lucien, before Jacquot, I thought of myself as Baron Rothbruce, of Currency Creek. That's in Australia. Never been to Australia, but neither had anyone else. Can't say I'm lying if nobody knows better. Marsupials were regularly compared to mammals. Fit the same niches, apparently. The same, but different. Normal, but weird. Not that I knew it at the time. Hadn't worked at the archives then, scanning, recognizing, correcting. I guess I should have said I was Rothbruce, instead of Jacquot. But Oksana's on the outside. She might have been to Australia. And I know better. Some clients didn't know they weren't kings, presidents, philosophers. A symptom of their condition, like laughing is, for a hyena. She's still sitting on the chair, lingering. I looked up. I'm going to say something.

Oksana says Polly is the generic name for a parrot. Polly wanna cracker? The name in context, I guess. Maybe I didn't understand Lucien, when he started calling me Jacquot, why he started. Everyone went along with it. I went along with it. It was easier. But I don't remember the anecdote. Doctor Wimsatt said I had a great memory. After she read the notebook. For having remembered so many animals, so many details. Unless I was making them up. I wasn't. I believed I wasn't. I'm not like the clients who mistake themselves for kings, the hospital for their kingdom. I know the difference. I just didn't understand everything. The banter seemed random. I knew it wasn't, but it seemed random. If I was that confused, the doctors would never have let me out of the hospital, the walls. I might be like my father, though. My father, his condition, confused the doctors. Over twenty years of confusion, even though each doctor seemed sure, of the diagnosis. Doctor Todd, his misshapen heads were sure I could make it at the archives. They were wrong. Yet knowing they were wrong would have been worse. Knowing they were wrong beforehand, I mean. Hold on.

Oksana says I'm stabbing the notebook with my pen. I need to calm down. She prefers Jacquot to Polly anyway. Polly's a stupid name. Who cares?, she says. Call yourself whatever you want. She's no longer sitting on the chair. She wandered off. I'm alone, to write, for the moment. Lucien was smart. He knew things beyond what we were scanning, recognizing, correcting. He had probably visited Australia. The records we had were old. That's why we were doing what we were doing. Jacquot was maybe the name for parrots fifty, a hundred years ago. Or it was the name picked up on a ship transporting the birds to the zoo. In a coal bunker, to protect them from the fog, wind. At sea, lots of birds were actually left free on the deck. They were happier out of a crate, couldn't fly all the way to land. A word like mtoto, repeated endlessly by locals on safaris. Abandoned by the time animals reached the zoo. It means baby, apparently. Used when young were spotted. Used when any animal was spotted once it became clear the white men would give them money for pointing out beasts to be captured. Maybe the foreigners wouldn't know the difference between young and old. Worth a try. Like at the hospital, the collectors favoured the young. Easier to move, crate, adapt to a new life. More years left in that life, if all went well. All told, the better investment.

Doctor Wimsatt no longer reads this notebook. I have to visit a doctor regularly, to check my condition, monitor my transition. More than one doctor, actually. I saw more than one doctor at the hospital. There was more than one nurse, keeper, attendant. Doctor Wimsatt wondered why I didn't write about them. Lots of animals at the zoo got to know their keeper. Elephants, bears, wild dogs, hogs. One observation stuck with me. A hundred observations stuck with me. This one just seems relevant, in context. Mary's little lamb followed her for food, warmth. If Mary had a pig, it might have followed her out of genuine affection. Genuine affection. I wrote about Doctor Wimsatt because she asked me to. Same reason I wrote about her bottle of gin. There's more I can say about Doctor Wimsatt. It makes sense to me now to write about her. Even if she won't read it. Unless I end up back at the hospital, and she hasn't retired. She did read what I wrote before I left, about sacrifices and sins. About The Board and Garbage Bin. About being on trial. She asked me if I was going to hold people up, with a revolver, on the outside. I said no. Then I had nothing to worry about, she replied. I don't believe it. Not exactly. But, sort of, I guess. I have a job, a place to live. I just can't screw it up. I messed up at the archives. She was willing to give me another chance, though. I can do it this time. Doctor Wimsatt said I wasn't missing anything by not understanding sins and sacrifices. Kids writing whatever the priest wanted to hear, enough sin to be believable, enough sacrifice to be good. Omitting, twisting, lying. Or being honest, and if I thought I would have a hard time on the outside. She paused right then, let her words trail off. I didn't really understand. I said so. She explained that it was like my father. They were trying to convince someone of something. If I didn't want to be like my father, I needed to use the notebook for something else. At the archives, I got lost, then anxious, then I acted out. As if I was an animal in a circus ring, nervous about all the eyes, staring at me, peanuts, being thrown. I should use the notebook to think through these moments, my emotions. Her suggestion, probably a good one. Not like Soko the chimpanzee at all. I don't think I'm stabbing the page anymore. Maybe it's working.

I agree, but. The archives replaced by a church basement. Clean, pleasant, stacks of chairs, boxes against the walls. Well labeled. Meticulous. Couldn't actually see the walls. They were there, probably painted. It wasn't the place for raw concrete. A piano, upright, on one side. A choir singing upstairs. And I agree, but. Repeated, endlessly. I understand the need, but. I respect the minister's decision, but. A good idea in general, but. My task was to record, organize, classify the eternal but. On a computer, on a table, at the edge of the room, by the piano and boxes labeled x-mas lights, bells, reindeer, nativity and more. Reindeer were imported by stores, malls for Christmas. Nobody thought about what to do with them after. Many ended up in the zoo. Didn't last long. Was curious what sort of reindeer were in the box, whether one had a glowing nose. Sometimes someone, a guest, a citizen, a taxpayer, sat at my table. Said what they had to say. I wrote it down. Mainly the people from the ministry dropped off sheets of paper full of scribbled lines, curves, dots. The archives scanner would have been completely lost. I was somewhat lost. I needed to check, see if I got it right. Normal, human. But then the computer corrected me, spelling, grammar. Sentence fragments. More aggressive than in the computer room. At least it seemed that way. I was anxious ministry people would see it, decide I wasn't good enough, send me back. I'm old, this could be my last chance. I'll pick up the technical language at least, of business, law, politics. The archives gave me some confidence. Import, export duties come up a lot. I already understand them. I wonder what duties reindeers had. Sudan had export duties for birds, $50 a bird. Expensive at the time. The basement felt like a crate. Some small holes worked in, but dark, enclosed. More than a cage, or a paddock. Maybe not a crate, but a hold, a coal bunker. The reindeer were in the crate. The voices above, the wind, brisk but not stormy.

Ministry people had magnetic name tags, with names, positions, departments meaningless to me printed on them. Far less useful than the labels on the boxes. One gave me a stick-on tag and a marker, at the beginning. I wrote Jack, stuck it on. Another set up the computer and, with another, explained how the session would go. I sat down, by the piano and x-mas boxes. People wandered in, filed in at busy times. Took in the displays. Maps on easels. The city as it is. The city as it will be once the surrounding land is swallowed up. Maps showing roads and rail lines, maps with housing and factories, maps with water and sewer lines. The river is always marked, the one detail relevant to everything, meandering from one corner to the other, all curves, no lines or dots. It took me a while, in between bouts of writing, on the computer, to find the hospital, where I was a client. It's going to be in the city, if the land is really swallowed. Doctor Wimsatt will be happy, her cottage less isolated. If Doctor Wimsatt can be happy, she might have landed at the hospital for the same reason as the clients. It's the only place for her. Only, it's worse. There's no plan for her, to rejoin society. The city will probably expand. It's what cities do. But the walls, the grounds, the buildings won't change, can't change. There has to be a place for people like my father to end up. Like me, maybe. Like Doctor Wimsatt, her bottle of gin, maybe. Not like Nurse Galverson, the keepers and attendants. They go somewhere else at night. The hospital isn't home.

Repetition in context. The names of the ministry people will eventually have meaning. I haven't written in this notebook for a while. About two weeks, I guess. Don't like putting dates in here, times. Reminders I'm getting old. I'm already old. Getting older, less adaptable, less worthwhile, closer to my father. Closer to the circus elephants sent to the zoo to live out their last years. Last time I opened the notebook, I wrote in my room, on my desk. The room was ready, the paint dried. My furniture had been moved in, I helped. Now I'm no longer in the hallway and my bedroom is also my writing room. At least when I write in this notebook. Most of the time, I write on a computer. Type on a computer is the common way of saying it. It's all writing. I prefer the notebook. It doesn't keep telling me I'm making mistakes, giving me suggestions on how to write better. I'm also not just writing what other people have told me or noted almost unreadably. Sometimes unreadably, I've given up repeatedly, in that context, to read notes. Sometimes I think maybe the archives computer would be better. In that context, which is not always a church basement. It's sometimes a school gym, with a maze of coloured lines crisscrossing the room. Each representing a different sport I don't know. A reminder of what I missed, growing up as an inmate, then a patient. And now it's too late, I'm no longer a child. I'm there to work, to write on the computer, by typing. I'm too old to play there. Halls, we also go to halls. The big business delegations show up at the halls, usually, file in. The maps are the same, the ministry people look the same, give me the same instructions. As if I hadn't heard them before, which is just as well. I may have forgotten, not understood. The context could change and I might not notice. All the rooms are large, have at most a couple of small openings, windows. They still seem like coal bunkers, even though most don't have boxes, crates. Or coal, I guess. It's still the same sort of people, stuck together until the journey's over, when they will probably be stuck in the limits of the city. I guess they sort of realize it already, most of them. They're arguing over the details. No, not exactly that. They're arguing they're exotic. They need special food, a special enclosure, special treatment. They're human-like in a better-than sort of way, in the opposite way than me. They deserve an individual name. Despite all their voices, their noise, it's hard to imagine the hospital for the less-than, where I was a client, not getting the most special treatment of all.

My room is white. George had it painted white. George runs the house, or manages it. Not sure what the difference is, though there seems to be one. Like the director and the head doctor at the hospital. The room's colour before it was painted was white. It looked off-white, because it was old. All the walls in the house are painted white, most of the ceilings, some of the floors. My writing room is now white. I suppose that is also a mist colour, more of a mist colour up in the sky, in the middle of the clouds. Vague objects wouldn't be mothers, sisters, but birds, planes. There are no cameras in my writing room now and I can close the door. I don't, though, close the door. At least not all the time. I didn't know it was good to have this notebook, supposedly of sacrifices and sins. I knew it was weird, to sit in the writing room, not writing. That was okay. It didn't cause conflict. Writing in the writing room was just better, I guess. Nurse Galverson gave me this notebook, she came into the writing room and placed it on the newly varnished table, in front of me, sacrifices side up. So that I had something to write in, she said. She never explained why the sacrifices side was up. I didn't look back, at her. I was looking at the blue-grey wall, then I was looking at the notebook. I didn't thank her, I should have thanked her. It would have been polite to have thanked her. After that, I still looked at the blue-grey walls, and occasionally at the small desks for children or little people around the edges of the room. Mainly, though, I wrote. The most appropriate thing to do in the writing room. I don't know what else I might need here, now that I have a notebook, and a pen. So I keep the door open. Maybe I do need something else. I don't know all that much. With the door closed, I might never know. George says I should write in the common room. George says all sorts of things that don't make much sense, things that give sense to the name George. That and setting up the room where I write. And laughing when he says something he realizes makes no sense. He laughs without shame, straight ahead. Doctor Wimsatt always turned away when she laughed, like it was unseemly. And cooking, he cooks dinner for everyone, to eat, in the common room. Hold on.

Oksana's perched on the edge of my bed. She isn't alone. Neither am I, now. Three people, including Oksana. She slammed a bottle of beer, already open, beside my notebook, on the desk. Then she perched herself on the edge of the bed. The others are leaning. I think they live here, in the house. I should write down their names. Soupy and Ham. That's what Oksana calls them. Not much better than The Board and Garbage Bin. But then Jacquot was taken badly at the archives, beyond the room where I scanned, recognized, corrected. Shouldn't judge, is what I'm trying to say. Soupy and Ham, and Oksana. And a beer, that I should try. God damn it, culture's been cancelled and now everyone's being mopey, is what Oksana said, when she banged down the beer, on the desk beside the notebook. I don't know what all that means. Seems to belong on the sins side of the notebook, if that mattered. Foam spilled out of the bottle, from being banged down. It is turning into liquid, approaching the notebook. It's all okay. I left the door open, I can't barricade myself in my writing room. It's all okay, except the puddle.

Culture is cancelled. The notebook did not get wet. I am still writing on the sacrifices side. Because the side doesn't matter. The beer was good, I guess. Beer tasting was not a life skill taught at the hospital, where I was a client. And I don't have much experience, with anything, outside. That the beer didn't have a label, an explanation, didn't help. They didn't stay long, Oksana, Soupy and Ham. People in the common room were mopey. I was boring. I have nothing to say. Better to just listen than ask or state. People get impatient when I ask, then loud and angry. Like I should know, should learn faster. I ask questions like a child, but I'm not a child. Not that everyone is patient with children. Not that Oksana, Soupy and Ham got angry at me. They were loud, angry, just not at me. At culture being cancelled, apparently. At the hospital, culture was a sort of skill. Recognizing it, mainly. Contributing to it, rarely. Lots of movies, TV. Kept clients occupied. They broke things down for us, too. Religion, politics. We wouldn't be at the hospital forever. Culture was one part of life the doctors couldn't control. It might knock us off our stable routine. To survive on the outside, we needed a stable routine. We needed to be numb to it, to the constant bombardment. Yet not completely numb, ordinarily numb. As numb as everyone, outside the walls. A sort of half-pickling. Fully pickled, we'd end up at the museum. With all the dead animals, the ones that didn't make it. If we were fully fresh, we'd be antelope. Skittish, nervous, anxious. With all the activity, the noise, we'd panic. Run into the fence, hurt ourselves jumping over it. Outside is just a collection of insides. Hurt antelope almost always die soon after. If they were special they'd be pickled. Most aren't special. Most culture, the doctors and clients could do without. Cancelling culture would be a relief, I guess. Was the archives banter so hard to follow because of culture? Did I sound like a parrot because I didn't get it? Is N'Gi's double boiler hat culture? I just don't understand enough. Doctor Wimsatt said I should use this notebook to work through my thoughts. Like my thoughts should be getting clearer, the more I write. But they're just getting more jumbled.

Start again. Culture is cancelled. Oksana seems to have meant shows have been cancelled. Theatre, exhibitions, that sort of thing. All over the place. So long as all over the place is just around here. Turn on the TV, the usual programs appear. The radio is still full of music and conspiracy theories. Stores, billboards, bus shelters still scream, cajole. No need to panic, try to jump over the fence. Unless you're an impala. They can clear any fence. And they should, because they can. I can say that, that there's no need to panic. Because of my stable routine. Clerk I, Special Opportunity Class. Special is less-than, in the context. Less money, modified duties. Still an opportunity. Churches, gyms, halls, every day. Not every day. I get days off. But I have a job to go back to, after the break. I write, type, on a keyboard, on a computer. I can sound like a parrot, like Jacquot, and it's okay. It's what I'm supposed to do. Repeat what people say, what they scribbled, the eternal but. The sense of what they say, note, doesn't matter. I still want to understand it, if I can. Which will come, with repetition, in context. Like at the archives, where I was a Clerk I, Special Opportunity Class. This is a better opportunity, I guess. For me, though I'm older now. Doctor Wimsatt, her bottle of gin, thought so. It's why I'm writing in my white writing room, in a rooming house. She knew about what happened at the archives when all this was arranged, approved. And I'm here. Shows, exhibitions are not part of my routine. If they are cancelled, it doesn't matter, to me. It clearly matters to Oksana, to Soupy, to Ham. They are not brown hyenas, not even as a loose analogy.

Halls. The big business delegations show up at halls, usually. They talk to ministry people. Everything, everyone seems interchangeable. I am a ministry person, but not really. Maybe when I get a magnetic name tag. Delegations don't have name tags. It's like everyone should already know them. Maybe the ministry people, the ones with fancy name tags, do. Other people don't have name tags, either. They come in as individuals. That's enough. Delegations are like herds, only better. On safaris, collectors spotted the young, the yearlings, the mtotos. They worked to separate them from the group, make it easier to capture them. Predators did the same, only included the old, too, and aimed to eat them. The suits delegates wore hid their infirmities. Their refusal to scatter, relying on the mass of the group, made them all seem strong, healthy. Age differences were obvious but meaningless. How they grouped together, who spoke when, the cards handed out, all that meant something, in context. It was all beyond me. Probably would always be. Even writing down the words said, the ministry people didn't rely on me. Maybe next time, one might say. Just listen for now, another would add. They never assumed I was hopeless, not exactly. At least, they never said it. There were just two classes of people. I was there for people who had trouble getting their words out, on paper. Few were actually illiterate. They just preferred talking, writing was a chore. Or, if they did write, it was a chore to understand, it was shaky, confused. Not nuanced, technical. It was often technical, I guess, just not hard to decipher because of that. At the archives, I was alone, not being able to follow the banter. I was alone, being from the hospital, as a client. Now, I'm lumped in with others. People who didn't go to school for very long, didn't do very well. I am the better-than of the less-than of the human-like. I interpret, as best I can, bridge the two worlds. It doesn't make sense. All these people rejected schools, institutions, or were rejected by them. They made their way on the outside. They succeeded, I guess. They're here. They talk about their business. A business they've run for years, typically. They know what the magnetic name tags mean, but will make do, accept me. Not as one of them, not as someone who understands. Just someone who records their concerns, tries to get them right. The minister will probably ignore them anyway. A comment often repeated. Never written down, except in this notebook.

The Chamber of Marine Commerce, Interior Navigation Section, today's grand delegation. If you're reading this, there are some things to know. Import, export duties. Duties are paid on pretty much everything going in and out of the city. Basins were built outside the city, warehouses, factories. All along the river. A lot of stuff arrives by ship, ends up sold in the city, a lot of stuff goes elsewhere, after being stored, transformed. The city is a big market and has lots of workers, makes sense to be close to it. An example. Wood is shipped down the river, ends up in a table factory, by the basin, just outside the city. They make a hundred tables. Half end up sold in the city, half elsewhere. The half going into the city pays duties. The rest, no. The project being discussed, why I have a job, is to expand the city. The delegation generally supports the project, but. But the new boundary would include the basins, warehouses, factories. Duties would have to be paid on all the wood coming in, and for the all the tables going out to be sold elsewhere. Basins, warehouses and factories can't be easily moved. Businesses can't afford the duties. So, there it is. The problem. The ministry people nodded a lot. Repeated the concerns, like Jacquot might. No solutions were offered, not there, not the time. Needed to hear everyone's concerns, present them to the minister, reflect. Other issues were mentioned. Taxes, fees, complications. Don't really understand them yet. It's like a magical ring just outside the city, where all sorts of things exist that could not survive anywhere else. A unique habitat with lots of fragile creatures impossible to keep alive in the city. Or at least challenging to keep alive. Like loons and grebes. Oksana, Soupy and Ham might be loons. Loose analogy, of course. I know nothing about loons. Only that they didn't last long at the zoo. And that culture being cancelled is somehow connected to the project.

At first, the maps confused me. I didn't know how things fit together. I knew certain locations, bus routes between those locations. The house, ministry office, doctors' offices, pharmacy, library, bank, other stores. Everything along route 52. A couple of blocks off, at most. Except my psychiatrist. Transfer to number 9 at Greenview. When I was at the archives, it was different but the same. Different buses, the metro to work, in the city. Same sort of locations. My life is pretty simple. The churches, gyms, halls are also different but the same. Coal bunkers. I show up at the office, above a mall, where a lot of the stores and the library are. I get in the back of a van, with the maps, easels and everything else. Ministry people get in, magnetic name tags in their pockets. One drives to the bunker. We arrive, everything's set up. I write, as needed, off to the side, on a computer. Then everything goes in reverse. I catch my bus at the mall, go home. The times change, the days. Halls, weekdays. Churches, evenings. Gyms, weekends. Not always. I have to pay attention. Bus schedules are different, weekends, evenings. I get anxious sometimes, check and recheck the schedule, go to the stop extra early, stand at the stop thinking about what I would do if the bus didn't come, if I missed it. Try sitting, but can't stay sitting. Too nervous. Then the bus comes. Not always on time. But it comes. And I'm okay again. Not as stable and routine as the archives. Not what the doctors at the hospital would prefer. I'm old, though. It's a chance, to be outside. After the archives, they didn't have to give me another chance. They could have decided I was like my father. Not suited for the outside.

I looked at the project maps, when I wasn't writing, on the computer. They started making sense. I found the hospital, where I was a client, on every one. Outside the city, a little forest surrounded by farms on maps with air photos. A little pink square labelled government, institutional or hospital on others. I like the trees better, as an adult. A cage is nicer with trees. At least when you've outgrown your fear of being eaten by a witch. I don't think I ever believed the stories, I was scared anyway. I knew the hospital was outside the city. It had to be. Clients are like wild dogs. Inapt to life in the outside world, dangerous to themselves or others. The zoo took in wild dogs as well, collected by the Biological

Survey or the Fish and Wildlife Service. The zoo was in the city. Not in the centre, just not surrounded by farms. The wolves taken in took well to their cage, the easy, regular meals. Weren't aggressive, difficult. But when the whistle at a nearby factory went off, they started howling, getting nervous. The zoo records labeled it Call of the Wild. A regular reminder of what was underneath. None of them were really tame. And clients' conditions never really go away, they're just managed. I manage my condition well, I guess. It's why I'm on the outside. I thought it funny, that a factory set off the Call of the Wild. Yet the city had its own sort of wildness, its own cruelty, savagery, indifference. And a factory was part of that. Violence controlled, channeled to break things down, mold them into something else. When I started to understand the maps, all that seemed wrong. Not completely wrong, just not right. The Chamber of Marine Commerce made it obvious. The factories weren't in the city. I guess some might be, but generally not. And I'm not in the city. Not me, not the house, the ministry office, doctors' offices, pharmacy, library, bank, other stores. Every coal bunker I write in is just outside. It looks like the city, there's no farmland in sight. That doesn't seem to matter. It doesn't seem like the city boundary matters. Yet every day I write how lives will be ruined if the line is moved.

The farmland is meaningless. The hospital is in the magical ring. It's a sort of factory, I guess. Breaking us down, molding us to sell us back to society. At a discount, Special Opportunity Class. The hospital's still different. I'm sure the tables from the table factory are first rate, each leg just as long as the others. It's just not that different. Not now. Maybe when I was an inmate or a patient. Maybe that's why my father never made it out. They didn't have the right tools. I've been worried about becoming my father. Maybe I've always been like him, only the world around us changed. Stuck with fairy tales and towering trees, behind a wall, time seemed to pass by, change nothing. Like the pills I take. The anxiety pill changes shapes, colours. It's still just the anxiety pill. The computer room came to be, somehow, I don't remember exactly how. It wasn't, then it just was. Yet we were still in the walls, with the trees towering over us. The head doctor changed, yet the resignation and alcoholism didn't. And the conditions remain. If the project goes ahead, pushes the factories and all the rest further out, replacing the farms, will it be like the zoo? The zoo walls didn't keep out the noises, of the urban wild. The hospital's won't either.

The manager of the Belleville Theatre came to the gym today. Made me think of Oksana, Soupy, Ham. I pass through the common room. I don't linger, except to eat. The house eats in the room, together. Like at the hospital, only less people, better food, fewer issues. Fewer issues than the house I lived in when working at the archives. I seem to be the only one from the hospital, and I'm good at managing my condition. And apparently the culture of eating with knife, fork, spoon, on plates, with napkins, has not been cancelled. I saw the three at the table, making protest signs. Against the project. Later, at the table, when the house was eating, multiple times, they brought up the protests. They had stood in front of the ministry office, marched between the office and city hall. They did things that I don't really understand. Performance-ins, guerilla-symposiums, culture-wakes. The moping seemed over. I didn't see them at the ministry office at the mall. They probably meant the main one, in the city. Everything seemed to happen in the city. As if cancelling culture in the ring just shifted it. It didn't really die. It was weird. They were taking their culture to the city to fight against the city being expanded to them. I just ate, listened. Best not to ask about any of it. I probably won't ever understand

and my questions could cause conflict, unnecessary conflict. They never bring up the protests in my writing room, perched or leaning. Oksana always leaves me a beer. Never slams it down, though. Not since the first time, when she announced the cancellation of culture. They never stay long, don't talk much, while I'm writing. I'm generally writing, in my writing room. Probably know I come from the hospital, don't want me to feel isolated. Don't expect anything from me. It's nice. Like the escaped cockatoos at the zoo. They just wandered from place to place, didn't really leave, always came back for food. Somewhat destructive, but nobody's perfect. The keepers never bothered recapturing them, didn't make sense. Maybe that's what I didn't know I needed. A regular reminder I don't have to stay in the cloudy mist of my writing room. I can leave. I don't have to leave. But I can, without running into a mess of overlapping made-up kingdoms. A regular reminder people capable of avoiding conflict can visit me. People who seek out conflict, just not all the time, not with me. Something to consider.

I didn't ask the manager of the Belleville Theatre anything about the protests either. He talked, I wrote. I confirmed what he said. Then he spoke with the ministry people, with the magnetic name tags, they shook hands and he left. Writing his comments didn't seem like it would have been a chore for him. He didn't struggle with words, expressing himself, was not a less-than. He just preferred talking, dictating. I was happy writing, even if it wasn't in this notebook, in my writing room. Kept my mind off the maze of coloured lines crisscrossing the room, the sports I never learned to play, and the security guard standing at the bunker entrance. There didn't used to be security, then there was. A little after the protests started. Just in case, I guess. Oksana, Soupy and Ham didn't mention violence, but it was probably there. The manager's name, Isidore Fresne. He began as most do:

He is in complete support of the annexation project of the suburbs to the city from a general point of view but he cannot but bring to the attention of the superior authority the prejudice that the measure will cause him in his situation, if certain concessions are not made. He has been the director of Belleville Theatre for almost five years and has made significant efforts to raise up an establishment that had never been able to stay open two years running. His rent increases every year and the municipality has just raised the good works tax fifty percent. The expenses are such that any additional augmentation would make the operation impossible. It is certain that, if he would be forced, like all the theatres of the city, to abandon an additional eleven percent of his gross revenue to the poor after annexation, there would be from his point of view a worsening of his situation. In addition, the commission for playwrights requires higher royalties for city theatres than those in the suburbs. It is not to fear, but a certainty that the commission will use the incorporation in the city to demand higher rates. It is in the interest of suburban theatres and young authors that the current state of affairs, as much in regards to the good works tax as to royalties, is not changed for at least five years after annexation. It would equally be necessary to allow suburban theatres to put on productions of the repertoire of the city stage, per the agreements currently in place.

His words, his sentences, his nuance. As I remember them, far from perfect. Don't understand it, not completely. More complicated than the table factory, I guess. A city theatre pays to be the only place in the city to put on a play, apparently. They pay more, get better plays. Or at least ones from better known playwrights. A suburban theatre does the same thing. Only they pay less. Pay less rent, lower taxes. But I'm not sure they do the same thing. Maybe they pay less for lesser known playwrights, younger playwrights. Ones that can't make it in the city, yet. People like Oksana, Soupy, Ham, if they were playwrights. They live in a house in the ring, with me. They can't be famous, rich. Have probably never been to Australia. Wouldn't make sense. And then fewer people see plays in the suburbs, pay less. Fresne didn't say that. Just an assumption, since we don't have much money, folks living in the ring who talk to me are scraping by. There's money in the factories, warehouses. Don't think that matters, in the context. If the suburban theatres were in the city, they would have to pay more, for everything. Everyone would have to pay more. So, less money to go to plays. More money going out, less coming in. But then, I don't get why Fresne said the suburban theatres put on plays put on in the city. That means they're paying for the same plays, just less. Plays from the famous playwrights. Only not in the city. Once they're in the city, they couldn't do that. A better situation for Oksana, Soupy, Ham, if they were playwrights. The theatres would be forced to put on their work. So long as they could stay open. Which is doubtful, according to Fresne. Royalties alone. Yet ring playwrights might not be able to live on the same money. Rents would go up, with everything else. I might be in trouble. Pay for a Clerk I, Special Opportunity Class does not go far. I don't understand what Oksana, Soupy, Ham are protesting, but there really is a lot they could protest. Even without the project. I wonder if all the managers, theatre and all the rest, cancelled the season, in protest. That makes sense, I guess.

After Isidore Fresne, other managers came. Some formed delegations, spoke with the ministry people with magnetic name tags. Some had statements already typed out. Some came to the edge of the room, by bleachers, stacks of chairs, pianos, and talked to me. The picture was filled in. I was right. Doctor Wimsatt, her bottle of gin, were right. This notebook is good for working through my thoughts. And the season was cancelled. In protest. It's still weird.

Cancelling culture in the ring, then performing in the city. Not the performance people want, not like the bears, always pleasing their audience. Grovelling, pathetic. But adaptable, hardy. Animals died because of visitors' food, given to them, thrown at them. Laurier, peanuts. At the beginning, people were used to circuses. Zoos were new. More animals for a smaller audience in circuses. At the beginning, the zoo didn't have rules. Animals died. Rules were set. Don't feed the animals. Behind the rule, another, not on the sign. If you must feed the animals, feed the bears. The animals that aimed to please could take the peanut onslaught. The ring is a unique habitat, with lots of fragile creatures impossible to keep alive in the city. Oksana, Soupy, Ham are not bears. Yet they're in the city, out of their element, performing. It's for the best, I guess, that they're not bears. Bears have been abused, more than most animals, historically, for fun. Still, weird.

I've been outside for a while. Not that long, but long enough, to think through some things. The misty walls of my writing room are still white. Maybe the writing room walls at the hospital, where I was a client, were blue at first. The blue-grey came with age. Another reason I felt at home there, perhaps. The white is good, too. A fresh beginning. But now I've been outside for a while. The routine is set. The house, ministry office, doctors' offices, pharmacy, library, bank, other stores. Travelling between them, regularly. I've visited more places since I was let out than ever before. Churches, gyms, halls. They're the same, not exactly, but effectively. Institutional. What the doctors, at the hospital, were looking for. Make it easy for me, to manage my condition. I've spoken with so many people. Actually spoken with people, normal people. People who didn't know of my condition, who assumed I was normal too. It wasn't real, I wasn't a person, not really. Just an extension of the computer. My task has been to record, organize, classify the eternal but. When I talked, I repeated what they said, scribbled. I was Jacquot and they were satisfied. Not really satisfied, not with the project. Unconvinced their words would reach, move the minister. Just satisfied with me, their expectations met. There was sometimes banter I didn't really understand, other subjects. Health problems, garbage collection, parking. Some would have liked me to take in everything, send it to the superior authority, have it dealt with. But they didn't expect it. It was normal to not follow the banter, to let it go, to only record, repeat the but. The banter between the magnetic name tags has been limited to the van, an occasional aside in the bunkers. Without the days spent scanning, recognizing, correcting, it doesn't develop, not really. Anyway, I don't have a magnetic name tag.

I can't explain it, I guess. Why my nervousness grew at the archives. I mean, I can explain it. I just don't know if the explanation means anything. It's all loose analogies. Human-like, stuck in my ring, expectations to perform. The audience feeling something between unease and dread. No exhilaration, it wasn't the circus. It wasn't a tent, but hard concrete blocks, sharp edges, conflict in waiting. Like the antelopes at the zoo, skittish, nervous, anxious. They panic, try to jump the fence. Fail, hurt themselves, die. Only some don't even think of the fence, jumping it. They run into it, break their necks. If they survive, they're put down. A loose analogy. Humans aren't put down. Except The Board and Garbage Bin, they were put down. Adults, less-than, a danger to others. I was just a danger to myself. The fence didn't feel a thing. Enough to end back at the hospital. Up to the doctors to decide, what to do with me next. Pills, therapy, life skills. And doubt, on both sides. After Nurse Galverson gave me this notebook, to write in, in the writing room. My thoughts had been lost in the blue-grey mist. My body couldn't pass through, but my mind could. Not much thought, meaning, like whatever was scratched in the table. My mind gets stuck on these pages now, is fixed in time, space. Lines, curves, dots. Repetition, in context. My thoughts don't matter much, though. They might, I guess. At least when Doctor Wimsatt read them. Maybe they're one reason I'm outside now, beyond the blue-grey walls, the pink square on the ministry maps. Don't know. In a way, the doubt isn't there, not for me. I knew about my father, the conditions the doctors thought he had. I decided to write them down, in this notebook. They are stuck now, fixed. I read them, reread them. Over twenty years, a condition that might never have been. Yet it always was, somehow, because my father was there, in the hospital. In the asylum, at the beginning. Written down, in his file, along with his plea. Written in a writing room, in a hospital, just before he died. I can't explain anything, but I'm not supposed to. It's not up to me. But there may not be an explanation, period. Just pills that change shapes, colours. Culture and life skills to chase after. I have an explanation. The ring around the city is like the circus ring. I'm somehow neither the performing animal nor the audience, but on the edge between them. It's lacking, my explanation. I mean, the hospital's in the ring, too. More likely I've just found another inside, with a writing room, where I write, in the same notebook as always.

All beavers need to lead a normal life is running water, mud, sticks. An observation from zoo records. I remember a lot of things from the archives because of repetition, in context. Some-times, it is something else. Something that sticks. Even if my head is mainly empty, a jack-o-lantern with a wavering flame. And now that it is written, here, it is stuck forever, fixed forever. For me. Running water, mud, sticks. One beaver made a hole in the fence, made it out of the zoo, cut down saplings, dragged them back for the dam. This went on for a while. Then, one day, it couldn't find the opening. No one was sure why. Made its way to a creek, then the river. Lived well, evaded capture. Until one day, an encounter with a farmer, a club, death. I would never have made that hole, would have panicked if I couldn't have made my way home, would not have lasted a day. Born into captivity, I need the inside. I feel anxious just thinking about wandering around the house. Like Oksana, Soupy, Ham. The cockatoos. I leave my door open, but I don't leave, not when I don't have to. Which is a lot. Feeding, defecating. Work, doctor's appointments. All of that planned, organized. The most basic life skill, taught at the hospital, organizing. I feel the most anxious these days waiting for the bus. I always think it won't come, I'll be stranded. Can't get rid of that thought, just manage it. Part of my condition. I admire beavers. They like insides, too. Constantly burrowing, building dams, houses, enclosures. But always escaping from them, wandering, discovering. Being free isn't needing the outside, it's not caring either way, being at ease wherever. The opposite of my father, me. I think I'll go for a walk.

Oksana, Soupy, Ham were in the common room when I went by. Oksana looked surprised to see me, outside my writing room, at that moment. I stated my intention. To commit myself to it, not just in this notebook, but to others. Ham replied that I wasn't fooling anyone, then asked Soupy if there was something he could do. Soupy asked me if I felt happy. I didn't know how to respond, interact. Oksana started laughing, a light laugh, before cutting it off, covering her mouth, apologizing. I guess I looked lost. I was lost. I walked out of the house, took the bus to the mall, bought a map. The map looked very different than the ministry ones, except for the river meandering across it. Running water seems just as important to people as beavers. Not sure about the mud, sticks. There was no line between the city and the suburbs, as if the project had already been approved. Or as if the city didn't care about the boundaries the government set. No sense of duties to be paid, the limits of the city repertoire. Places of culture were marked. Belleville Theatre, lots of other theatres, museums, galleries. I guess culture is a thing. Even if it's been cancelled, it's left its mark. A thin line of blue leading to the curve of the river was the closest water from where I stood, at the mall. A canal. A beaver would head to the closest water, so that's what I did. Carefully, my thumb on the map, marking my movement. If I didn't lose myself on the map, I wouldn't be lost, not really. Find water, go home. That was the plan. A beaver would follow the water. I wasn't ready for that. Between the mall and the canal, everything seemed old, and just got older. Or just dirtier, dustier. Greyer. In reality, not on the map. My father died at 32. He was ancient, broken. His plea desperate. 32 passed me by and I am still younger than him, on my way to become him. I might have been dead by now, if I was still in the hospital, as a client. Spending so much time in the writing room, the blue-grey walls ever greyer. A different grey than at the archives, worn, ready to give way, fall apart. I wasn't paying much attention, to the world, just made sure my thumb kept moving on the map. Streets noted, but I couldn't write a single name now, not from memory. Doctor Wimsatt would have scolded me, ignoring so much of what's around me, right there. Then a truck, a big truck with a big trailer, went by, thundered by, and the air was suddenly grey, a mist of grey between me and everything solid. I started coughing, couldn't stop, couldn't stay on my feet, leaned against a wall. Eyes watering. Sat down on the sidewalk, against a wall. Stared into the grey, lighter grey as the dust settled. It was just dust. I repeated that, to myself. Just dust. Another truck. Squeezed my eyes shut, held my breath. Just dust. I was anxious, panicky, I could feel it. But I'm good at managing my condition. And I did. My hand ached. The map was crumpled, but my thumb stayed, still marked where I was, in the world. Wiped the sweat running down my face, like mud on my hand already grey with dust, from the wall, the ground. I looked around, noticed that the grey of the buildings around me was like at the archives. Hard concrete, strong. Metal dulled, dirty. Somewhere along the way, rundown houses were replaced by factories, warehouses. I hadn't noticed. Until I was sitting on the sidewalk. A sidewalk that felt like a ledge, the trucks so close. Moving seemed like too much risk. I'd fall off. I'd die. I didn't want to die. I'd just sit there, be smothered with layer upon layer of dust. Anything to not be hit by a truck. Managing my condition is so much holding on. Let the panic wash over me, through me, let it attack me, and hold on. Because it'll pass, if I hold on. It always passes. I just need to hold on. And I did, with my thumb stuck on the map, crumpled but readable. And, slowly, I was okay. No thoughts of beavers, of running water. Just the house, my writing room, white like clouds.

One of the ministry maps shows houses and factories. That's the map I need. No, I just need to find a bus to take me to the river. And maybe walk around the block, find a park. Write down options, better options. Plan, organize. And don't be paranoid. Oksana, Soupy, Ham didn't know what was going to happen. They weren't being mean. They didn't want to hurt me, see me hurt. Oksana apologized for laughing. Jacquot was a light-hearted observation. Lucien was nice, not cruel. Still better no one was in the common room when I came back. So I could be alone, even before I closed my door.

I never thought about going into the city, myself. It wasn't something to avoid. It might be something to avoid. All the people, movement, chaos, conflict. The archives are in the city, it wasn't a problem then. The problem of the archives was the inside, not the outside. And me, my condition. The city did seem like a problem, once. The Call of the Wild, set off by the city, wild dogs reverting after acting so tame. Me, effectively a wild dog, unsuitable for society, a danger to myself or others. I might have hurt others at the archives. I wasn't thinking when I hurt myself, I don't remember exactly how I hurt myself. I woke up in the hospital. Not the hospital where I was a client, a regular hospital, I was called a patient. I was broken. Badly. But they were able to put me back together, physically. And when I was on the mend, physically, they transferred me back to the hospital where I had lived, before the archives. The hospital where I had been a client, and was once more. If I was an antelope, they would have put me down. For a while I wished I was an antelope. Then I was on the inside, at the hospital, and I wanted out. Like my father. Unlike my father, Doctor Wimsatt thought I could do it. Her and her bottle of gin. My condition is still inside me, better to avoid what makes it harder to manage. I knew from the ministry maps, the trigger may not be in the city. The factory whistle is usually in the ring around it. I knew that, I guess. On a certain level. Then I went for a walk. Without thinking. Or thinking about beavers and not what was really around me. But it's good. I learned. I survived, without help. No hospitals. I managed my condition. With the pills, the therapy, I'm never really alone. Even if there are no cameras in my writing room. I'm still a patient, maybe a client. Not really sure. I never really wrote about Nurse Galverson, never got to know her. My fault. I appreciate her, for this notebook. I thought about Oksana, Soupy, Ham in the city. Protesting in ways I didn't really understand. Still don't. And now they've asked if I want to come with them, to the city. Not to protest. Not to seek out conflict. Since I was leaving my room now. Not just for work, obligations. Going for walks. I've been going for walks, to the park. Even went to the river, once. On the bus. Should go back. It was nice. I didn't see any beavers. Lots of mud, sticks. Large trucks, looking small, on a bridge in the distance. I'm going to say yes. I need to say yes. I need to trust them. I can't let here become an inside. At the hospital, they teach clients that we need to interact with others, to fit in outside the walls. I'm not sure I care about fitting in anymore. I don't really want a magnetic name tag. I just want to interact with Oksana, Soupy, Ham.

Culture was not cancelled in the city. Or maybe it was. I wouldn't know the difference. Still not sure exactly what culture means. Even theatre, exhibitions continued. According to the ads in the metro, massive ads curving with the tunnel. Maybe culture was replaced, though. Waiting for the train, at a station in the ring, not yet in the city, hieroglyphs curving over us. Egyptian, an exhibition at a museum, in the city. Here isn't Egypt. Egypt isn't the Egypt on the wall, ceiling. It's somewhere else, another time. Culture, sure. Just not this season. On the train, when it came, small posters, things to buy, see. Plays, movies among them. Can't tell if they're like the Egypt display, like reruns on TV. Maybe there's enough culture stored in the places of culture on the map that a cancelled season doesn't matter. Go back five seasons, or three thousand years, people will have forgotten, the details at least. People don't really forget the pyramids. Still worth seeing again, people will pay money. It'd be cheaper to put on, don't have to pay the author again. If I understand correctly, if the rights last. First time I've been in the metro since the archives. It hasn't changed, I have. Beavers, I tried not to think about beavers since the trucks. They had come back, to mind, when I was by the river, with the mud, sticks. But I was underground, in a metro station, then in the train. Other animals burrow, tunnel. A couple of cats were on the Egypt poster. I couldn't remember if beavers were a thing before, when I was at the archives. I couldn't remember if the platform seemed like a ledge, a narrow ledge, when I was taking the train, to work. The air the train pushed in front of it, through the tunnel, sweeping the platform, was so clear, it didn't seem right. My skin felt dust I couldn't see, wasn't there. The tunnel was its own world, an inside in the outside. The train was a relief, protection. Nicer than the bus, smoother, simpler. I had more confidence, that it would show up, that I wouldn't miss it. Wished the house, ministry office, doctors' offices, pharmacy, library, bank, other stores were connected by train, underground. The train only goes to the city, is a tentacle of the city. Speeding along in the tunnel, in the car, filled with people and ads for things to buy, see, I wondered where the line was. The line the government set, between the suburbs and the city. The line the city didn't care about, on the surface. People were silent, except Oksana, Soupy, Ham. Staring off into nothingness or at their phones, the solid ground all around us a giant screen, people projected whatever they wanted. If the tiny screen wasn't enough. Everyone a store of culture absorbed, living their lives outside, in the world.

Soupy was saying the movement was changing. It's what movements did, Ham replied. Oksana agreed, if it wasn't changing, it was dead. What they were saying kept slipping away. The movement was the protests, I guess. Probably the performance-ins, guerilla-symposiums, culture-wakes I didn't understand, didn't really care to. Death wasn't just farmers, clubs. For beavers. The zoo had trouble getting them in the first place. Too valuable as pelts. All the trappers, all the traps, killed them, maimed them. Took a special effort, to find someone able to capture them alive, unhurt. The deaths at the end didn't matter much. There were always births, babies. Beavers lived well, in a cage, with running water, mud, sticks, so they bred. I could have said that. Something like that. The movement could die. So long as it left little ones. It would die, eventually. No matter what they did, how it changed. Focus on what comes next. Wouldn't have mentioned the beavers. Didn't say anything. Wouldn't have been a repetition, wouldn't have been Jacquot. Not any better, though. Maybe if I'd paid more attention. Doctor Wimsatt said I should. I should write about the people around me. I should think about the people around me. Being there was hard enough. Interacting by being there. A long way away from the writing room, at the hospital, alone. A wall between me and the brown hyenas, laughing, because that's what they do. Still. Soupy, short for Soup Bowl. The shape of his belly. More insulting than Jacquot, if Jacquot was insulting. Everyone seems okay with it. Soupy's okay with it. So, I should be, too. Ham, short for Henri-Mathieu. Easier to say, I guess. Oksana's Oksana. I'm learning, a little, by being around.

The rest of the trip was cut up, grainy. Mist, dust, shades of blue-grey, washed out in the white clouds, how I usually see things that aren't clear. The bunkers have been clear, the routine, the repetition, in context. Doctor Wimsatt, her bottle of gin, Doctor Todd, the skulls, misshapen. Other things, real, imagined, all hazy, regularly hazy. Coming out into the city, the middle of the city, from the metro tunnel, was clear, solid. I'm sure of it. Evening, light fading. Still, enough light to see clearly. Lights are everywhere, in the city. But it's torn up, in my memory, writing about it, in my writing room. Torn up, cut up, grainy, it's all wrong. Hard to find the words. I'm pretty good with words. One of the reasons I'm on the outside, despite my condition. A life skill. Later, we saw a bunch of films, experimental, Solomon Nagler. They've infected my memory, or enhanced it. Changed it. But not that of the trip to the city, in the train. Just there, in the city, everything was something. Grainy, cut up. And multiple exposures, people around me moving, staying put, all at once. It would have been terrible, the city like that, being in the middle of it. Even with Oksana, Soupy, Ham, anchors to context, the house, routine. Writing, in my writing room, in the clouds, afterward, searching for words, it's manageable. Words. Self-hatred is the best foundation for self-examination. From the start of a film. The Sex of Self-Hatred. Wasn't that film, coming up the metro stairs, into a plaza, concrete, but softened, worn, young people lingering, talking, gesturing, overexposed blotches of white, splotchy more than grainy. Others, older, better dressed, quickly passing through, golden tinges. Men, with shopping carts, garbage bags full of cans, moving slowly through. And staying still, ghost-like. Not many of them, but leaving so many traces of themselves, everywhere, despite themselves. Like the plaza's defined more by their presence than the others. I followed Oksana, Soupy, Ham through the images, afterimages, suddenly our own little delegation, cohesive, stronger together.

The light abandoned the sky, fell to earth, drowned the street. So many colours. The people we passed took them on, richly. And they were painted, dark lines, curves, dots, setting off spines, elbows, anywhere bones could pop out of glowing skin, fabric. The restaurant, we went to a restaurant, to eat, drink. Could have been a café, wasn't paying enough attention. More colours, shadows. Crowded, bodies bent around other bodies, distorted. My memory wants to cut it with the man, the self-hating Jew, alone in the ruins, a gun in his hand, pointed at his head. But it doesn't happen. Instead I see Susan Buck. Not bending, but gesturing, talking, drinking, eating, at a table, with people. Plain light, dimmed, directly overhead. They looked normal, doing what people do, in a restaurant. I stopped, then was pushed along, by Soupy, who was behind me. He wanted to find a table, start doing what normal people do, in a restaurant. And we did. Doctor Wimsatt, her bottle of gin, said I should work through my thoughts, feelings, in the notebook. Now I'm outside, now she doesn't read it. I felt something, when I saw Susan Buck. My mother's social worker, back when my mother had a social worker. When I was born. Afterward, too. Don't know how long. Don't know my mother, never knew her. Never met her, after coming out of her. Everyone has a mother, I guess. But I don't have a mother. It's why I'm at the house, with Oksana, Soupy, Ham. Nor a sister. Just the fact of it, my situation. No blame, anger. No point. Susan Buck, I know. I knew. And I felt something, when I saw her, recognized her. She hadn't changed much, from a distance. I guess I felt old, burdened. I feel old, usually. It's just time doesn't weigh on me, it's behind me. My condition weighs on me, but there's no real difference between me and my condition. Managing my condition is managing me. I just felt heavy. I don't know how to work through that. It was nice to be with Oksana, Soupy, Ham, at a table. The plain light, dimmed, directly overhead, made us look normal. Us fragile creatures from the ring, in the middle of the city. I had the same beer Oksana ordered, which came with a label. Don't know anything about beer, though at least this one had a name. I only know the ones she's brought to my writing room, when I'm writing, are good, though anonymous. And we ate, outside the house. Even under the plain light, the beers glowed slightly, amber, a tiny candle at the centre of the table added occasional flickers before sputtering out, bodies kept moving, bending, at the edge of my vision.

Most of the words on the screen, spoken, written, I didn't understand. Hebrew, Polish. Jewish images, I recognized some of them. Ham said Nagler was Canadian, based in Winnipeg. More foreign culture, I didn't think where it came from mattered. It seemed important, somehow. Not important like hospitals, food. It just had something to say, show. Worth seeing, listening to. Better than the fog, unvarying fog. Objects, people unfocused, not really there. The film burned, it looked like it burned, for a moment, the white revealed was clarity, not cloud. The textures, scratched, cut up, grainy, added to the world. I think, sometimes, my pills and the fog are the same. Not that simple, I guess. If the outside was sharper, harder, conflict would follow. Best to avoid conflict. Sort of. That's not so simple either. Stopped for another drink after the films, they were all fairly short. Ham talked about the odd life of Otto Weininger, the self-hating Jew. Killed himself at 23. Bullet to the heart, apparently, not the head. Talked technique, Nagler was old-school, whatever that means. Ham's a filmmaker. I didn't write that down yet. And enjoys foreign culture, put on in the city. In the middle of a protest. Soupy asked me what I thought. I replied I had to think about it. He pushed a little, asked me if I was good with it, if the images weren't too disturbing. Seemed odd, to ask afterward. Too late to be concerned. An episode, incident would have happened already. If it was going to happen. The soft blue-white light of the bar, dark furniture and walls were pleasant with the extra texture I was seeing. I wasn't really seeing them that way, I don't think. It's just how I remember them. I was fine, I responded, to Soupy. My gin and tonic was glowing. Oksana had ordered a gin and tonic. I did the same. It glowed more than the beer. The only thing that wasn't rough to the eye. There was a suicide watch, at the hospital, where I was a client. I was never on it. The closest I'd come was at the archives, I guess. It wasn't suicide, attempted. Any more than an antelope running into the fence would be. Just tend to hurt myself more when the world around me is harder, sharper. If that's what Soupy was referring to, the gun to the head. There were lots of images, references. I didn't get a lot of them, numb to others. Spending so much of my life in a hospital, as a client, patient, inmate. The context, repeated, is tics, urges, manias. We walked back to the metro, crossed the plaza. Some of the men with carts were sitting, at the edges. Fewer young people, still gesturing, smoking near the centre. Don't recall if they were smoking before. They seemed louder, bigger. A police car slowly passed by, marking the presence of order. Everyone playing ordinary, normal roles. Even if it's weird the homeless, cops, seemed normal. Down the stairs, the textures were lost to lines of bright fluorescent lights, leading us to the train.

Susan Buck. Don't want to write about her, not today. I know the night with Oksana, Soupy, Ham was good because I forgot about her. Until I started writing. I felt heavy, then it went away. Didn't even have to hold on. Just be pushed a little, by Soupy. And I left the beavers behind. I like the beavers. Clerk I, Special Opportunity Class, feels less-than, sometimes. Running water, mud, sticks puts it in perspective. I wonder if my father had a shopping cart. He lived on the street for a while. Before convincing the doctors, police he was a danger, to himself or others. He could write, I saw what he wrote. It didn't matter. I don't really think about the end of the bunkers, writing people's issues. A decision has to be made, about the project, eventually. Maybe there won't be another special opportunity.

Had dinner, at the house, in the common room. Oksana, Soupy, Ham weren't at the table. They sometimes aren't. I wasn't, once. They were in the city, protesting. As they do. I said something, at dinner, to George. Everyone seemed surprised, that I said anything. As they should, I guess. George said he wasn't concerned. The three knew what they were doing, weren't alone. Others spoke, my concern became conversation. The movement had changed, apparently. Suburban culture was cancelled. For reasons Isidore Fresne and others told me, the ministry people with magnetic name tags. Those affected protested the project. Then suburban students protested the protests. City schools are more respected, better funded than those in the ring. Marine Commerce and rail unions joined, against the project. Workers from factories, warehouses followed, starting with those reliant on river and rail shipping. City businesses, complaining about unfair tax advantages in the ring, followed in opposition to the opposition. The most recent player, siding with the suburbs, is the Liquids Market, all the wine, liquor, vinegar wholesalers serving the region. Apparently every player changes the rules, the game. Jumping from one colour to another in the gym. The conversation continued, everyone except George backed their favourite. It was all meaningless. Everyone just as ignorant as me, everyone shouldn't be as ignorant as me. Not supposed to be how this works, on the outside. The only things clear, performance-ins, guerilla-symposiums, culture-wakes can't be everyone's approach. Nobody was moping anymore. And I'm here, writing this, in my writing room.

SINS

And the true point of my life is perhaps only this: that my body, my sensations and my thoughts become writing, which is to say something intelligible and general, my existence completely dissolved in the head and the life of others.
Annie Ernaux, *Happening.*

The words above were already written. By Nurse Galverson, probably. I mean, by Nurse Galverson in this notebook. Apparently by Annie Ernaux, originally. My body, sensations, thoughts are symptoms of my condition. My condition is the diagnosis in the heads of my doctors. It could also be real. No one can decide. That was true in the hospital, I guess, where I was a client. I don't know if it's true here. I don't know how Ernaux's words are sinful. Maybe the sins side was just facing up, when Nurse Galverson needed a place to write the quote. Now that Doctor Wimsatt doesn't read the notebook, I don't think anyone does. Gin was the only thing that dissolved in her head, in any case. Intelligible and general. Generic, Jacquot. Repetition, in context, what I hear, see, remember. I'm good with words, should be intelligible. Otherwise I wouldn't be going from bunker to bunker, writing. Wouldn't be outside. The hospital as a factory. I have other skills, life skills, writing concerns is what sold, what the ministry bought, for now. I've read Annie Ernaux. Parts of a book, maybe some books, sent by Susan Buck. When she sent me books. And letters. I didn't have a mother, sister. I had Susan Buck, for a while. My mother's social worker. Everyone has a mother, I guess. But I don't have a mother. Susan Buck found a way to come for a visit once or twice a year, for a while. She would never have prepared a landing pad for me, when judged ready to leave the hospital. She wasn't my mother, no mistaking it. If she was, maybe I would have lasted longer at the archives. No blame, no anger. Just something that might have been different. When I was an inmate, books didn't last long. Not much of any value to anyone lasted long. And I was small, afraid of everything. I read, repeated, remembered what I could. Words, lines, out of place, context. I wrote the words, lines, in my letters, to Susan Buck. Proof I was reading, asking for more. The books didn't matter, didn't really understand what I read. Needed the context, I guess. Even then, I might not have understood. No, I just wanted someone outside to send me things, to care enough to send me things, with my name, my real, actual, individual name on the package. It made me feel less small, though just as afraid. I was almost proud when the bigger boys, men took the books, ripped out the pages. I fought at first, didn't last long. Just gave up when the boys came, gave them everything, easier that way. That I had something of value, worth destroying, was something. I was already broken, worthless. But I didn't hate myself, wasn't like Otto Weininger the self-hating Jew. It's all weird, in memory. Susan Buck, why I'm pretty good with words today, better than the average client, at the hospital. Maybe they have Annie Ernaux, at the library.

I've made it to the sins side. No more room for sacrifices. I'm writing in a hospital, a hospital for patients, in the city. Maybe the one they took me to, after the incident, at the archives. I don't remember. It's weird, to be at a hospital, and not be a patient, client. To be at a hospital for someone else. It's weird to write outside a writing room, surrounded by people, people waiting for other people, people the people waiting care about, or for a nurse to call their name, to see a doctor, have their condition treated. I see doctors regularly, in offices. There are people there, nurses, but it's not institutional, not really. And I never bring my notebook. Oksana, Soupy, Ham weren't at dinner, at the house. George wasn't worried. So, I wasn't worried, at first. I was worried, that everyone around me seemed as ignorant as me, but not about Oksana, Soupy, Ham. I was still thinking about them, wrote about them, not being at dinner. Then I pulled out my map, crumpled, worn. I had gone to the city, the river, the park. Outside continued to be outside. The routine of the house, ministry office, doctors' offices, pharmacy, library, bank, other stores, continued. It's just my life was more than that. Just not so far as to risk running into a farmer, a club, death. I found the ministry office, in the city, city hall, marked on the map. Not places of culture, but of government. I guess government isn't culture. They were the places protests might be, if the movement hadn't changed too much. I would visit them. If I saw Oksana, Soupy, Ham, if they were alright, that would be good. I don't think I saw or smelled anything, from the house to the metro station. Definitely didn't, following the lines of fluorescent lights, standing under the curve of Egypt, staring at the dark walls, through the reflections, as the train carried me into the city. Looking up the stairs into the plaza, the exit was blocked by an orange-brown wall. I stopped, people bumped into me, not hard, everyone saw it, at least slowed down. Someone commented she didn't think the fires were this bad. Another said it looked apocalyptic. Apparently there were fires, so the orange-brown wall wasn't a wall, not a solid wall. I shifted to the edge, against the side wall, people flowed around me, accelerating, like they needed to punch through, rush through, hurry to wherever they were going, minimize time spent outside, exposure. I stood there, against the side wall, the flow slowed, stopped, then started up again, another trainful. My eyes followed them, other dark shapes in the haze, moving, disappearing. Real, they were real and the wall, in front of me, wasn't. I didn't feel anxious, panic, didn't have to hold on. It was like I was back at the hospital, in the writing room, before

Nurse Galverson gave me the notebook, sacrifices side up. I just stared at the blue-grey wall, through it. Time passed, it didn't matter. The routine would catch up to me, I'd follow it, as clients did. I thought things, but they weren't fixed, not like when I started writing, in the writing room. Another wave of passengers went by. A transit cop went by, came back, asked me if I was okay. I didn't answer. He asked again. I nodded. He shrugged, made a comment about the fires, the smoke. Chaos, he said. The protests had gotten out of hand. I imagined Oksana, Soupy, Ham, dark shapes in the haze. Then I went back down, back to the ring. A thought stuck, even without writing it down. Planned, organized. I wasn't organized, I needed to be more organized, needed to plan.

When I stared into the orange-brown again, hours later, I had a mask over my mouth, nose. I had a bag on my back with water, food, goggles, spare masks (they came in a five-pack), notebook, pens. Don't know why I included the notebook. It just seemed important. Now, here, waiting in the hospital, it's good I have it. I can work through thoughts, feelings. As Doctor Wimsatt suggested. Though I'd have preferred reading Annie Ernaux, understanding the quote better. It felt off, someone else's words in the middle of the notebook, not written by me. I also had names. Oksana Blackburne, Galen Lord, Henri-Mathieu Claudel. The waiting room is full. People are talking about the smoke, fires. Everyone seems to be here because of the smoke, fires. I already had a plan, I guess, the first time I faced the orange-brown wall. Visit the places I knew protests had been. It just seemed to be on the same level as walking to the canal, as a beaver might. Barely a plan, a less-than plan. But I was learning. I might have gone out into the smoke, before. Choked, panicked. Instead, I retreated, eventually, thought things through. People passed through the plaza, quickly but not too quickly. No one lingered. Even the homeless had found a better place to be, it seemed. But maybe they hadn't.

Don't really know. They just weren't there, in the plaza. My thumb on the map, crumpled, worn, I moved slowly, carefully forward. I knew I wasn't in a wall, it still seemed like the haze could become solid, at any moment. It wasn't reasonable, maybe a symptom of my condition. But I wasn't in a hurry, once I had the goggles on. The mask worked well. The ministry office, in the city, was across from the archives. Streets seemed more familiar as I got closer, while staying alien. Benches, trees, garbage cans had been burned. The sidewalk sometimes crunched underfoot. Buildings loomed, black. I couldn't tell if they had been touched. They were standing, at least. My footsteps crunched more and more. Couldn't see anything at first, then noticed it was broken glass. From bus shelters, but more than that. Bottles, labels scattered here and there. They hadn't burned, seemed odd. I recognized Doctor Wimsatt's gin, but not Doctor Todd's whiskey. Shards were sometimes darkened, blood probably. Not a lot. Fences had been put up, in front of the office, archives. Police, with masks, shields, batons, lingered. Nothing green, living remained on the grounds around them. Everything that was going to burn had burned, making the smoke still in the air seem out of place. The line of flagpoles, usually flying government flags, was bare. Some of the windows were filled with boards instead of glass, or over the glass.

I stood there, between the office and the archives. Something had happened, a battle, I guess, but not to the death. Except for the trees, flowers, grass. Not enough blood for human, animal victims. It seemed over, An occasional person or small group entered, exited the buildings, showing badges to the lingering police as they went by. Work continued, life continued, human life, on the inside. A small group passed right in front of me, headed to the archives. My eyes followed them, imagining them in the hard, sharp maze of concrete, working, existing. It took a moment to recognize Lucien and the rest of the group assigned to scan, recognize, correct zoo records. If they were still assigned to that. The work might be done, was probably done, they'd moved on to other things, without me, in the same building. I felt invisible, behind my mask, goggles, comfortable watching them, faces uncovered, hurrying inside. No stories, banter was important enough to open their mouths, not out here, in the orange-brown haze. An officer broke off, approached me, told me to move along. Nobody remained from the conflict, no Oksana, Soupy, Ham. Assuming they were ever there. So, I did. Move along. My thumb following along, on the map.

The road to city hall was usually full of people, on foot, in cars. Lounging, lingering on patios on the wide sidewalk or crawling along, bumpers inches apart. The cars were still there, adding to the haze. The patios were gone, windows boarded. The unburned wood contrasted with the scorched trees, all along the boulevard. Should have been the opposite, if I understood the rules. The trees didn't hurt anyone. It was city businesses protesting the tax advantages of the suburbs, those of the suburbs protesting the monopolies of city businesses. But I didn't understand, didn't understand much of anything. The smoke shrouding buildings in the distance, the monotony of the empty sidewalk, the line of boards, everything made the street feel so much longer than I remembered. I guess I walked it before, when I was at the archives, or even before that. I usually didn't walk further than the nearest metro station. Didn't go to restaurants much, linger on patios, interact, despite what I was taught, at the hospital, where I was a client. There was one, a station entrance, when the station thought came to me. Could have descended, taken off my mask and goggles, come up at city hall. For some reason, I kept walking. Despite the empty sidewalks, boarded up businesses, I was convinced there was more of a chance to run into Oksana, Soupy, Ham on the surface, outside. It didn't make any sense, I didn't really know either way. It was like I wanted an endless walk, in the haze, indistinct objects in the distance. A dream from the hospital writing room come true, passing through the wall, comfortable behind my mask, goggles, comfortable I wouldn't come out on the other side, find myself in a room with other clients, their tics, urges, manias. Higher chance the smoke would become grainier, sootier, the film would catch fire, disintegrate. So many things I impose on my memory, as I write it, fix it, in this hospital waiting room. Turning it unintelligible in the process, I guess. Just don't know if my life's unintelligible, or my writing. If I'm like my father, my life is a series of diagnoses, contradictory, a condition that may not be. My writing may be a plea, just for nobody in particular. Doctor Wimsatt already decided to let me out. Her and her gin, bottles of which had fueled the chaos, in the city.

I was not invisible, behind my mask, goggles. A police car pulled up beside me, flashed its lights. I turned, saw the driver's side window down, driver beckoning. I walked over. The officer asked for ID. I gave it. He looked tired, his partner looked tired. He asked me to take off my mask, goggles. I told him I had trouble breathing, with the smoke. He told me to get in the back. I did. He closed his window. Air was a bit better in the car, he explained. Then looked at me, waiting for me to take off my mask, goggles. I understood, after a moment. And did. The partner spoke up, said it was just a precaution, with all the vandalism. The group, torching everything, wore masks. Torching everything caused all the smoke. Because of the smoke, more people were wearing masks. After checking my ID, looking at my face, they didn't ask what I was doing there, where I had been when everything had been burned. Don't know why, maybe because I'm old. A human thing, I guess. At the zoo, apes went bad when they got old, lost their playfulness, their patience. Elephants, too. Kashmir deer and gnus were mean, violent all their lives. But I was human, in the back of the police car, without my mask, goggles. Or maybe there was a record of the archives incident, my history of living in hospitals, saying I'm a danger to myself, not to trees, flowers, grass. I felt human enough to state that all the fires I'd passed were out. The partner replied with a booming laugh, filling the car. Would have filled the waiting room, I'm sure, and all the way down the hallways lined with stretchers. If only the brain trust from the Liquids Market didn't think making Molotov cocktails out of their products and throwing them at everything in sight was the best idea since fermented bread, he continued, the laugh still echoing. If only they limited themselves to government buildings and didn't throw a dozen or so into the river valley for good measure. They started a wildfire in the middle of the city, my goggled friend, and it's still burning. It's not likely to be put out before taking a bunch of mansions down with it. I'm sure I got that right, the last thing the cop said right then. The language was confused, the sense clear enough. I thought of the beavers, first, though all sorts of animals were probably hurt. My mind kept coming back to them. Then that the movement had changed a lot since the performance-ins, guerilla-symposiums, culture-wakes. Might not have been the same movement, but one of a litter of baby movements. Young, human, violent. The original movement could be dead. It wouldn't matter so long as it reproduced, in the cage of the city. Like beavers, a loose analogy. The laugh was gone, the words hung in the air. The driver sighed, said they were going to city hall, if I wanted a ride. I accepted. The car crawled forward, like the one passing the plaza the night of the Nagler films, marking the presence of order. I didn't miss the mask, goggles, as it turned out. I wasn't really invisible. All three of us stayed silent, scanned the outside. Them for suspicious activity, me for Oksana, Soupy, Ham. None of us found what we were looking for as we entered the square, before city hall. A small crowd occupied a small area, at the far end, before a fence and lingering cops with masks, shields, batons.

Another baby movement, perhaps. Nobody was doing much, as if the haze had stifled all the energy, everyone reduced to dark outlines massed together. The car stopped at the edge, the partner let me out, telling me to stay out of trouble. The words made me feel young, then very old. I thanked them for the ride, barely mumbled it. Neither appeared to hear, had already moved on, mentally, physically, crawling forward, scanning.

My throat, my eyes started to get irritated, my body reminding me to put on the mask, goggles. At the hospital, as a client, I had to remind myself, when meeting with doctors, of how many clients they regularly saw. It was easy to forget, for me, meeting one on one. After the session, I went to life skills training, the writing room. They met with five more of me, conditions to be diagnosed, managed. They remembered some things, had notes in the file for all the rest. I tried to imagine how many people the cops had stopped, IDed, this shift. Maybe I was the only one they gave a ride to, but they still had to move on. Doctor Wimsatt probably remembers me, or would, in context. But I'll fade, quickly enough. She'll have to look at the file for everything. I'm sure I'll remember her, for as long as my mind holds. Even if Nurse Galverson hadn't given me this notebook, if I hadn't written about her, her bottle of gin, if she hadn't asked me to. She's just too important for me, my life. Doctor Todd, too. And Susan Buck. In the end, it was the hospital factory that molded me. Like the orphanage, The Board and Garbage Bin. The head doctors are molded, too, only in a way that makes them unsuitable, for the outside, for other hospitals. They're not witches, couldn't be with the children taken away. The cottage, partially hidden by the trees, still transforms them. A fairy tale ending in resignation, alcoholism. Police regularly come through the waiting room. I see them, sometimes, when I look up from the notebook, take a break from writing. They linger long enough to have a word with someone, a nurse, a doctor, a patient, then move on. They don't wait. Always someone else to see, to talk to. There's security here, on the inside, to crawl along, scan, provide the presence of order. Maybe should have asked the cops, in the car, who gave me a ride, about Oksana, Soupy, Ham. Doesn't matter now.

Mask, goggles on, at the edge of the square. I saw a small mass, constantly moving, crisscrossing the space, making a vague noise. It got closer, a giant vacuum, a small car. Not really a car, maybe a tractor, not a tractor either. Don't have the right words. Keeping the square clean, apparently. I took a couple of steps forward. No crunching. A priority, I guess, to keep the square clean, in front of city hall. Higher profile, higher standards. The state house's probably the same way, in the capital. A symbol of order, good government. Not our saying, I don't think, still not alien, to our culture. Keeping the ground clean, the people on it orderly. Can't do anything about the sky, the smoke, can't bring the trees, flowers, grass back to life. Powerless to stop the spread of the haze, outside. Probably blanketing the suburbs, too. I didn't notice it, when I went back, to get more organized, but it keeps moving. It looks solid, but it's not. I know that. I approached the mass at the far end, at the fence. Signs stuck up, couldn't read them, not yet. Without the crunching, with the hum of the vacuum, I felt ghost-like, insubstantial, in a different way. To myself, rather than to others. The smoke was more real, heavier. I wanted a breeze to come up, carry me off with the orange-brown haze. Like the white clouds of my writing room, where I usually write, only somehow more fitting, now I'm on the sins side of the notebook. The signs came into focus before the people. No More Second Class Citizens. Equal Education Opportunities. And more. Pro-project students from the ring, I guessed. Don't understand all that much, but that seemed clear. Closer, the mass came apart into people, more or less distinct. Young, though they looked older, through the haze.

Skin I imagined clear, bright, tinted an unhealthy orange-brown. What I imagined kids who worked in factories would have looked like, back when kids worked in factories, back when people like me were inmates, in an asylum. Hysteria isn't what it used to be. I felt like a cop, scanning the crowd, only the cops there, with masks, shields, batons, seemed indifferent. If no one crossed the line, the fence, they didn't care, I guess. Different than at the archives, where I was told to move on. Different rules here, maybe even a different game. No baby movement setting things on fire, people weren't crossing the square to go to work, get on with their lives. Likely the hall had another entrance, less symbolic, more practical. Oksana, Soupy, Ham were not in the group. Didn't think they would be, given the signs, the words written.

I was getting nervous, in the middle of the square, behind mask, goggles. I felt alone, exposed, that there was too much space around me. It didn't make sense. The smoke was still there, as solid as haze could be. A moment ago, I longed to be swept up into the orange-brown cloud, to lose contact with the ground. Before that, I was comfortable, enclosed, behind my mask, goggles. Then everything changed, without anything really changing. The square wasn't that different, and it was where I was supposed to be, planned to be, when I left the house, decided to come to the city. I brought my hand up, the one with the map, worn, crumpled, with my thumb following where I was. There was no map, not in my hand. It was gone. Somewhere. The hum of the vacuum suddenly seemed sinister, fading in and out, behind me, erasing all traces of my passing, everyone's passing, everything. It shouldn't have seemed sinister, a clean slate meant less conflict, chance of conflict. Best to avoid conflict. I was convinced it had sucked up the map. And it seemed I was in the square, before city hall, but with the smoke, I couldn't be sure. Walking toward the building didn't seem like a possibility, not really. I would just be going further from where I last knew I was. I didn't belong out-side, I couldn't survive, everything was wrong, Doctor Wimsatt was wrong, all the doctors were wrong, it was so obvious. Just look at what they concluded about my father, his condition, over twenty years. They didn't know anything. It was the gin talking, just like it was the whiskey and the tiny misshapen skulls that de-cided I belonged in the archives, full of raw concrete blocks with sharp edges. It's hard to write this, to work through it, in a waiting room. People around me, people outside too long, without masks, goggles, wheezing, coughing. The smoke they inhaled coming out into the room. I'm not alone, I can't close the door, the walls are a white greyed with time, scraped by stretchers, wheelchairs, all manner of things for the sick and damaged. I'm calm enough, good at managing my condition. I've thought it through, probably left the map in the cop car, on the seat. Don't know, never will. The most probable, is all. And I was at city hall, the square in front. Of course I was. The cops dropped me off there, the ones nice enough to give me a ride, some time inside, away from the smoke. It wasn't planned, I wasn't completely organized. I thought I was handling it well, I was handling it well, until I wasn't. But that passed, too. I just needed to hold on, and I did. Only this time, I had someone to lean on.

Safaris. To capture animals, alive and dead. For the zoo, but also for the museum. Both alive and dead were considered import-ant. Not like beavers, when the zoo was getting started, only val-ued for their pelts. The process was also important, the process of collecting, trapping, hunting, killing. They liked recording every-thing, thoroughly, but especially for exotic animals. It was always exotic animals when it came to safaris. So they didn't just pay for collectors, trappers, hunters, but also movie men. That's what they called them. Movie men. Just one, usually, on an expedition. Not a Hollywood production. Lots of stories, in the written records, written about movie men, their equipment, so much equipment. The film was digitized, too, but I didn't do that, when I was at the archives, never saw it. From the written records, it didn't seem like there was a lot to see. Lots of film, just not all that much capturing animals, being captured, alive or dead. When Ham appeared beside me, seemingly out of nowhere, I didn't understand what was happening, at first. I didn't panic, any more than I was already panicking. I just sort of looked at him, holding his phone hardly visible with all the accessories attached to it. It was pointed at the vacuum, tracking it. With all the smoke, my shots are going to come out like Nagler's, without even trying, is the first thing he said. Grainy, as if they could have been taken a hundred years ago, he explained. I registered the words, as I had gotten used to doing in the bunkers, storing them to be processed, understood later. Insofar as I could. And that was it, nothing was wrong anymore. Ham was there, beside me, confident he was where he was supposed to be, knowing exactly where that was, in the middle of the empty space, filled with orange-brown haze. My thoughts stopped spiraling, even if I couldn't yet get ahold of them, control them. I didn't wonder how he knew it was me, if he knew it was me, behind my mask, goggles. I never asked, likely never will. It just was. Then he moved, took in the group of pro-protesters, the fence, the police and the blurry outline of city hall, a building that was, in fact, there. My mind started processing, finally, and I thought of all the crates or equipment Ham didn't have to carry with him, all the organizing, planning necessary for the safari movie men he could do without. And yet it felt like the situation hadn't changed, not all that much. Safari movie men were almost always too late to capture the moment, of the capture. It took too long to set up and collecting was unpredictable, being in the right place, at the right time, reacting quickly. The small, sluggish group, the police lingering, the vacuum erasing, the trees, flowers, grass blackened. It all seemed too late. The real action had passed when everything was on fire, the square carpeted, with broken glass.

The monologue continued, the filming continued, I followed along. I know it wasn't his most technically or philosophically interesting film, but I'm very fond of Untitled 1. It's the one with the temple on the prairie, the buggy being driven along straight, flat prairie roads and shots of old farm buildings. It was winter but not too snowy. It was shot in black and white, and the snow on the ground pulled out the dark lines of the power lines and roads. Patches of grass sticking up above the snow shaded the fields in places. You remember it? Of course you do, we didn't see that many films that night. Everyone talks about Fugue Nefesh, The Sex of Self-Hatred and Black Salt Water Elegy. They have a lot more to say, no doubt about it. They have stronger themes and bring up some really difficult topics, so it makes sense. But there is something about the straightforward simplicity of the visuals of Untitled 1 that really works for me. Now forget about the snowy prairie and focus on the regular movements of that vacuum-thing. Look at how the signs are waving slowly, amplifying the subtlest movements of the protesters holding them. Look at how the metal fence the police put up reflects and concentrates what light there is and appears better defined than everything around it. Since the protests started, every group that has joined the fray has tried to outdo the last. In a couple of months, things have gone from peaceful marches and education campaigns to trying to burn the city to the ground. It's easy to get caught up in all that. TV crews are going around as we speak recording the most alarming and apocalyptic images they can find for the evening news. Videos of death and destruction shot years ago halfway across the planet are being posted to the web this very moment with claims that that is what's happening right now, where we stand. And don't get me started on artists doing stupid stunts to try to claim the avant-garde. It's worth holding back and taking in what's around us in an uncomplicated way, whether it's a snowy Manitoba prairie or our smoke smothered city. At least that's what I think, for what it's worth. Because you asked.

I hadn't asked. He knew I hadn't asked. Tracking a herd of gnu for days, but that day, after hours crisscrossing in front of the straight line of collectors and ninety local boys, the animals turned and ran straight at them. The boys ran at the herd, shouting mtoto, mtoto! The herd veered, right into a muddy-bottomed lake, They struggled out of the mud, but were already tired. By the time they were back on dry land, four young had been captured. Alive, destined for a trip in a crate, in a coal bunker, to the zoo. No one knew the herd was going to turn. Luggage was thrown to the side to prepare for them. Much of it ended up in the lake. The movie man didn't have time to set up, record the action. The equipment was dry, though. So, he set it up. And they let one gnu up, to throw it again, tie it up, this time on film. There was only enough rope for three. The one let up had to be tied with sturdy rags and a belt. The main collector's belt. Only the throw went badly, the gnu escaped, taking the belt with it. The movie man filmed a fake capture that wasn't. The first story that came to me, from the archives, scanning, recognizing, correcting. I imagined a TV crew getting a bad angle on a thrown Molotov cocktail, asking the protester to throw another, but to wait until the camera was better positioned. Maybe with a hazy skyline in back, giving the act context, in the very image. No need to explain, just a moment to recognize, realize this was happening in the city, close to home. But not too close to home. It was still a safari, the protester was still exotic, needed to be. Otherwise it would be boring, no one would watch. If they weren't human, they might be found at the zoo. Not so much circuses, not anymore. They could still end up behind bars, just not where curious visitors were all that welcome.

Though maybe it's all too much, now the orange-brown smoke is everywhere, outside. Maybe the exhilaration of circus-like danger has made way for a feeling somewhere between unease and dread.

Which doesn't mean this is all there is, Ham said, after capturing the sense of the square. If you have nothing better to do, come along. I found the dull M at the edge of the square, at least I think I did. Metro signs were usually backlit, at night. I'm sure this one had been, but it wasn't night, not really. Home, I could have gone home. I hadn't even looked for the station, earlier, before I had Ham, to lean on. Ham the movie man, his phone hardly visible with all the accessories attached to it. No crates of equipment, reels of film. Not an accessory to collectors, trappers, hunters. Master of his own movements. Still seeking the exotic, a sense only possible with the orange-brown haze, protests, broken glass to clear away. Exhilaration in his voice, when he described the waving, reflecting. Straightforward, simple, but not totally different. The fires had gone out, but it wasn't too late. The safari, a loose analogy, the latest in a long series. I looked for the M first, my first reaction, that I did have something better to do, retreat to my writing room, surround myself with white walls. Better to be somewhere I could manage my condition, I needed to manage my condition if I was to stay outside, not find myself back in the hospital, as a client, perhaps for good, like my father. The contradiction was not lost, even then, in the square, behind the mask, goggles. Needing an inside to stay outside, but then no longer being outside. I didn't have the map, but I had Ham. Only then did I think of looking around, for Oksana, Soupy. I had assumed they were there. In my mind they were always together. They were always together, when I saw them. Oksana, Soupy could have been in the smoke, dark outlines, but there weren't many dark outlines, the square was almost empty. The vacuum-thing, its driver, chose that moment to be satisfied with the tidiness of the square, headed to the fence. The lingering police made a break, the thing disappeared behind it. The emptiness became even more tangible. Oksana, Soupy couldn't be there, not right there. With Ham, there had to be a connection, to finding them. With Ham, I could be outside, my condition would be manageable. He had been waiting for a response, if I was normal I would have already said something. There wouldn't be a mass of thoughts, fixed as words, written in this notebook. I nodded, fished a mask out of my bag for him. We left the square, together, masked.

A better analogy, Ham as the gnu herd. Zigzagging, changing direction suddenly, shaking off the collector, trapper, hunter. Only there was no one following, tracking. We weren't exotic enough, worthy of individual names, if we were caught, ended up in the zoo. We weren't a large enough herd, a group with mtotos. Gnus were antelopes, acted like antelopes. More the brown hyena than the baboon. Ham was still dodging something. The predictable, perhaps, the staged. All the while searching for green pastures, under the orange-brown sky. Which also wasn't quite right. Antelopes in the zoo did not mix well with green grass, apparently. Ham was looking for something. When he explained it, it was obvious. When he didn't, it felt more like chasing shadows in the smoke, shadows without objects. I was better off without the map, no way my thumb would have kept pace. I tried to shift my thoughts, from the zoo, the safari, to Untitled 1. It didn't work, nothing was open, straightforward, not to me. Block after block, some crunchy, some boarded up, some with blackened trees, flowers, grass, we moved, maybe even progressed. Some roads were full of people, in cars mainly, going wherever they were going, life continuing along, headlights pushing the haze away more than slicing through it. Others were empty, abandoned. Nothing was consistent, not like the road between the ministry office, city hall. Chaotic, to me, but maybe straightforward, in reality. I didn't understand much, which was normal. The one thing consistent was the sirens. Didn't pay attention at first, couldn't hear them at the square, before city hall. Don't remember when they started. When they were there, though, they were always there, a layered discord from different sources, cutting through from different directions. Something was still happening, beyond the wall of smoke, in the wall of smoke. Where exactly was beyond me.

Roads curved more and more, as we continued, shops became rarer, houses bigger. Ham paused more, at intersections, avoiding increasingly common cul-de-sacs. Zigzagging was okay, not backtracking. I wondered if gnus would know to avoid the dead ends. Probably wouldn't seem like dead ends, the fences between houses not being much of an obstacle. They weren't like hippos, who tended to shy from even the flimsiest of fences. Or humans, who would shy from the invisible line, of private property. Ham spent less time peering down cross streets, though, and more up, into the haze. When I finally understood, I looked up, too. Yellow lights, accented here and there with red, blue, blinking, gyrating against the orange-brown. A sort of curved non-block later, we came across a line of trucks, flatbeds, pickups in front of a row of mansions. Landscaping equipment poked out the back, of the pickups, the flatbeds were empty. A rare police car here and there added contrast. No one was around, emptier, eerier than the square, before city hall. With the lights, signaling to nobody. Ham's phone, hardly visible with all the accessories attached to it, took it all in, the patterns, rhythms. Then he said they're all around back. He understood, I didn't. We crossed, on private property, through a fence, between two mansions. And suddenly there was noise, bobcats clearing a line of all vegetation, people in hard hats, vests, planning, organizing, digging, moving furniture, ornaments, pulling down fences. All in front of a mass of green trees. The river valley, I realized, after a moment. Everything was still alive here, the trees, flowers, grass. Except what was being cleared to dirt. It seemed absurd, to kill more, destroy more. A man with a hard hat, vest came up, asked us who we were, what we were doing there. I expected a cop to question us, didn't see a single blue uniform. The only uniform was the hard hat, vest. A uniform I didn't have in my bag, didn't plan for.

It was a fire break, to protect the houses, if the fire got there. The man talking to Ham was happy to explain the situation, especially when Ham convinced him we weren't media. Didn't care we crossed the fence, were on private property, weren't wearing the uniform. The work was happening, as planned, just a precaution. So he had time to chat. They didn't expect the fire to spread here, to this section of the valley, south of the Whitaker pipeline right-of-way. If the wind changed, though, it could. The forecast didn't predict it, but they could only trust forecasts so far. If the fire did come, they'd have limited options. The slope was stable, but not that stable. If they dumped a bunch of water here, it could give. Especially if the vegetation on the slope was burnt up, not holding the soil. Ham asked about clearing the vegetation to create the break, wouldn't that cause problems. Probably not, the man responded, but if the forecast changed to rain. He didn't finish his thought. It was clear where he was going, even for me. I wished I had my map, to see where the right-of-way was, put everything in context. It seemed like something found on a ministry map, though, not the one lost, probably left in the cop car, on the seat. And here I was, in front of the river valley, the one common feature, meandering across all the maps. I took the bus to the valley, before. It was open, easy to find, full of trees, life. Not like the canal, hidden among factories, warehouses. Had we not crossed the fence, gone into someone's backyard, I would have never guessed it was here. On the map, if my thumb had followed my movements, I would have seen it, not the actual trees, forest. On paper, just not in reality.

Ham asked about the people living in the mansions, whether they were still there. The area was under voluntary evacuation, was the reply. And most people chose to not be there. Not just because of the threat to their houses, though. They decided to skip the protests, the orange-brown sky, all of it. Made things easier, for the landscapers, not being watched while they were tearing everything up. That's why the police were there, to patrol, make sure there weren't any break-ins. In response to Ham asking whether we could walk along the break, the man said he wasn't going to stop us. It wasn't a controlled construction site and the fire wasn't all that close, at least not yet. He wouldn't advise it, either. Then he shrugged, went back to organizing, directing the work. It seemed to me we shouldn't be there, not really, but that the rules were in flux. Two backyards down, we'd be someone else's problem, five and we'd be lost, in the orange-brown haze.

I'd never been in a house as big, fancy as the ones we were passing. I'd never been in backyards so elaborate, every patio passed through a world in itself, stones, furniture, plants, barbeques. It was all the same, basically, yet somehow not. As if every owner gave instructions, to whomever was doing the work, that it needed to be different, better than the neighbours. The mansions, their backs at least, seemed more constant. Make it stately, the instructions might have been. And I guess everyone had pretty much the same idea, what that meant. They wouldn't have been out of place, behind the walls, at the hospital. The patios would have been unthinkable. I liked walking through the torn-down fences, solid walls removed from my path. The grey line of the break, curving along the edge of the valley, gave our path, a non-path in the grass beside the grey, an endless feel. Or, circular, if we walked long enough we'd end up where we started. Ham zigzagged, in the limited space, always finding things worth capturing. The situation had flipped from being too late, in the square, before city hall, to being too early. On a safari, it would be the moment the movie man would set up, lie in wait, for the animals to come. Before the first cry of mtoto. Close enough to impending action to record it, far enough to let the collectors, trappers, hunters act. The wind shift seemed somehow inevitable, the battle between flames and people fated. So much anticipation for so little, a couple of living trophies crated, out of hundreds in the coal bunker, on the ship, for the zoo. The hazy air was evidence the situation, there, then was not that different. So many encounters already passed, so many to come. Not all resulting in an antelope running off, with the head collector's belt, destined to be remembered. A tall fence appeared out of the smoke, in front of us, blocking the break. Closer, it looked like a cage, chain-link. Closer still, a tennis court. A patio of sorts, elaborate in its own way. Another game I didn't know how to play. The rules were probably easier than the games played, on other patios, where the lines weren't plainly painted. The break broke, continued again, on the other side. I wondered how the cage compared to bear cages, when bears were status symbols for the rich, when bear-baiting was the game to play.

We passed by, continued along. Yellow lights followed, above the mansions, accented here and there with red, blue, blinking, gyrating against the orange-brown. Not always there, but regularly. Men, women in hard hats, vests glanced at us, nothing more. I guess since we were already back there, not crossing, on private property, through a fence, between two mansions, we seemed to belong. The looks bothered me, I didn't belong. If anyone had challenged us, I would have broken down. Writing in the waiting room, in the hospital, looking back, my unease strikes me as human, remarkably human, for me. No physical barriers, no stated rules, yet I understood, at least somewhat, at least picked up something. Ham's presence, his confidence, his phone hardly visible with all the accessories attached to it, helped me on. I hadn't stopped leaning on him, not really. All the while, the Call of the Wild, in the city, took on a different form. The wild dogs that ended up at the hospital, as clients, were people. People who hurt themselves or others. A factory whistle started the dogs, in the zoo, howling. For clients, there was no end to the possibilities, triggers. For me, there was no end to the possibilities. Conflict, of course, There was always conflict, for me, with my condition. That doesn't mean much. The project, protests, for some. The protests splintered, the movement multiplied, conflict was sparked. Don't know how, when. I imagine not a lot of people paid attention, until the sky turned orange-brown. Conflict between order, Liquids Market troublemakers. Those hurting themselves, others, were still human. Maybe potential clients, maybe not. Depended on their condition. What doctors, judges decide, after the fact. Then the form shifted. Marketers started it, it seems, throwing cocktails into the valley. And they lost control, the fire in the bottle, released, did what fires do. The break wasn't against the marketers, but the fire. The creature in the ring, the cage was something I hadn't thought about before, made loose analogies about. There had always been a line around it, meandering across all the maps. Nature in the city, exhilarating usually, now stirring a feeling somewhere between unease and dread. In all this, I'm part of the audience. I have never been part of the audience. One of the reasons I felt I didn't belong, I guess.

We found the intersecting line. Whitaker pipeline right-of-way, Ham declared. It was cleared, easily three times as wide as the break. In front was a short barricade, a fence fit for a hippo. It worked, we didn't cross. Might have been more the call, by someone in a hard hat, vest, to not cross it, as we approached the line. Across looked at first like death, not just the trees but the abutting mansions black in the orange-brown haze. Red lights blinking, gyrating replaced the yellow in the sky. Staring at this new wall, it seemed to glower. There was a sort of life, smoldering, reserved. Ham looked fascinated, behind his mask. Since the square, Ham looked fascinated by everything. Maybe I'll understand better later, after seeing what he filmed, put together. Don't have high hopes. I never understand all that much, even less what I saw in Nagler's films. Ham's could be different, though. I have more context, it would be a sort of repetition of what I had already seen. The intersecting line cut down the slope, back up again, into the neighbourhoods on either side. I could finally see the decline, potentially unstable, the man in the hard hat, vest had talked about earlier, to Ham. And I understood it, better, still not perfectly. A wide, paved path went straight down the middle, in front of us, then curved, disappeared. On the other side, up the incline, the path, likely the same, switchbacked, in and out of the clearing, only straightening, settling back into the middle, near the top. The valley, adapted, for people. After staring, contemplating, filming, we crossed through a fence, between two mansions, to the street. Another barrier awaited, blocking the road, with a police car, a cop, an empty SUV with a network logo written down the side. Behind extended a row of fire trucks, firemen, spaced out, disappearing around the curve. The same curve, we hadn't walked far enough, for the valley, the river, to meander the other way. It just seemed different, with the mansions burnt, the red of the lights, the trucks. The road was the break from here on, the first row of houses belonged to the creature, in the ring. Unlike the trees along the pipeline, though, the houses weren't smoldering, reserved. They were really dead, carcasses.

Oksana's parents' house is up there, Ham said, nodding up the street. At least I think it is, it doesn't quite look the same anymore. I was almost expecting it to be the only one standing, perfectly pristine, with a phalanx of private firefighters guarding it, ready and willing to lay down their lives for the cause. The cause, my dear Jackboot, is to prevent the insurance company from having to replace it and all the priceless shit inside. I bet they never thought the art they were buying was ephemeral. Ham didn't seem to like Oksana's parents. Which means he knew them. Which means she had parents, has parents. All that seems obvious, now, in the hospital, waiting, writing. Then, in front of the barricade, it was a surprise. Clients had mothers, sisters, who wrote, received emails, visited once or twice a year. Even the movement, like beavers, had young before dying off. Still, when I came to the city, to find Oksana, Soupy, Ham, they were a group, impossible to separate, for me. They were always together, in the house, when they passed through my writing room, like cockatoos, when watching The Sex of Self-Hatred. In the square, before city hall, Ham was there, appeared there beside me, recognized me behind my mask, goggles. It took me a while to adjust, to accept him, alone, save for his phone hardly visible with all the accessories attached to it. That meant Oksana, Soupy could be alone, too. I had taken the group apart, in my mind. Then I had to stick it back together again, with other pieces, other connections, other people. Everyone has a mother, I guess. A father, too, sort of. It was just not something I imagined, for the three. I couldn't imagine Doctor Wimsatt as a mother or sister, either. The only thing she nursed, was her gin. They had their role, in my life, in the house, nothing more. Not even their real names. Without all that, if there wasn't more, maybe I wouldn't be so different, lacking, a The Board, Garbage Bin, Jacquot. The cop at the barricade, lingering, overheard Ham's words, asked if he was talking about the Blackburnes. Ham was suddenly shy, shrugged. It's poetic, if you ask me, the policeman continued, leaning on the barricade. We hadn't asked. He knew we hadn't asked. The Blackburnes own the biggest distillery in town, I don't know how many calls I've responded to year in, year out where the perp's drunk off Blackburne hooch, causing a ruckus.

Half the duty dodging, more than half, comes from smuggling that very same hooch. And now, now it's the fuel that's burning our river valley to the ground, the crown jewel of our city no less. But at least their pretty little house went up with it. Poetic, is what it is. Now if only they'd take the hint and move on or retire or something. If they survive, that is. They? Ham asked, softly, behind his mask. That's what happens when you think you're better than everyone else. You think you're above mandatory evacuations. You think the fire wouldn't dare touch your house. You think all the firemen in the city have no higher priority than to serve you. What you were saying, about the private firefighters, only it looks like they were too cheap. They thought being rich and paying taxes gave them claim to a miracle or three. They got one, they're probably going to survive. I heard it was because of their daughter, who let the firefighters know her parents were still there, refusing to come to the door no matter how hard they banged on it. The miracle was that they have a kid who cares.

A nervous energy, the policeman was giving off. The energy of someone stuck next to the fight, just not in it. Idle, powerless, trying to stay alert, always needing to be alert. Keepers, attendants got that way, sometimes, in the hospital, on long shifts monitoring clients, conditions. Conditions all too real, always unpredictable. On safari, too, lying in wait for the animal, exotic and dangerous. I liked that he spoke, I learned things, about people, the outside, Oksana. I assumed she was the daughter. Now, in the hospital, waiting, writing, I know she is. A miracle. Her parents could have died, like the movement, beavers. They weren't necessary, not anymore. But they were important to her, their daughter. She had parents, as people do, but she actually had parents, has parents. There's no question now, they're going to survive. I was also uneasy, that he spoke, in his blue uniform, surrounded by orange-brown smoke, to strangers, behind masks. I was uneasy. Ham was uneasy. The cop should have told us to move on or asked to see our IDs, faces. I write that now. Standing there, before the barricade, I just felt what I felt, absorbed his words. Processing, understanding, comes later, writing, in this notebook. Following Doctor Wimsatt's suggestion. Ham processed, understood quicker. Recovered his usual assurance, what I took to be normal, for him. Asked if they were at a hospital, which one. Asked about protesters, looting, thugs. The cop didn't know much more, it turned out. River valley, good. Alcohol, bad. People living in mansions, arrogant. His one job, don't let anyone unauthorized past the barrier. The network SUV was empty, hadn't paid attention, with the policeman venting. Scanning for the crew, they seemed to be at the far end, interviewing, filming. Shapes blurred by the orange-brown haze, I didn't really know. The only thing I felt sure, they were allowed past the line, to be part of the show. We didn't get past, didn't try, just moved on.

Out of sight of the barricade, cop, activity, we stopped. Ham stopped, next to a utility box, red lights still blinking, gyrating, above. I followed his lead. The Blackburnes own the biggest distillery in town, the cop had said. I wondered if that meant the factory was in the city, that the Call of the Wild, here, now, wasn't in the ring, the suburbs. Ham was unstrapping his phone, the mic, stabilizer, lens, put them in a line, on the metal cube. Far more the safari movie man, with his equipment in pieces, unable to react, film, capture quickly. His phone, suddenly a phone once more, stayed in hand. The houses around us were intact, unconcerned with the drama, around the corner. Couldn't see anyone, in the windows, probably empty, evacuated. Still, without the camera, after the camera, it was no longer clear we were the ones observing. He tried contacting Oksana, no luck. He moved on to people I didn't know. I don't know anyone, almost anyone, outside but not really interacting, not like we were taught, at the hospital, as a life skill. He texted, called, the feeling of being observed, windows themselves as eyes, increased. A police car crawled by, patrolling, marking the presence of order. Didn't stop, I expected it to stop, the driver to question our presence, a rule I thought I'd understood. Ham found what he was looking for, the name of the hospital, Saint Luke's. He strapped the accessories back on his phone, I sighed in relief. Back to normal, what seemed like normal, filming, recording. Not waiting for action, staging the action, just recording what was, in the orange-brown haze. Ham moved differently, though, zigzagged less. The houses we were passing, the curved streets, had started to repeat, I guess. And now we had a destination. He didn't say anything, he didn't need to, I just understood. I was proud, of myself.

The rings, cages, who's in, who's out, who's performing, who's watching, it's all complicated. The valley, fire, break, was simple. The zoo, circus too. Ham and I, we were coming up on another line, another barricade, more cops, more cars, this time at the entrance of the neighbourhood. Police lingered, watching us, behind our masks, all of us inside the line. They didn't move. Or, they did, slightly, subtly, the movements Ham loved to capture, with his phone, hardly visible once more with all the accessories attached to it. We came to them, passed them, found ourselves outside. I thought I was already outside, with the orange-brown haze. But I wasn't, not entirely. Looking back, toward the barricade, it seemed poor, disorganized, between stone walls, projecting strength, starting on each side of the road, continuing through the curve, into the smoke. Vista Verde, in gold letters, attached to the stone, on each side. Flowers, grass, colours muted but obviously not blackened, at the base. Strong, exclusive, but not brutal. What I understood, what I still understand, in the hospital, waiting, writing. An SUV, large, white, pulled up to the barricade, as we were leaving. The cops started moving, a couple actually approaching, the others straightening postures, looking more professional, alert. I looked back several times, as we walked, curious. A wooden barricade, part of the overall barricade, was shifted, the SUV passed through. A police car, another part, followed it, into the ringed, walled interior. I was born into it, the walls, the institution, not like this. Maybe like this. I wanted out, was scared to be out, found myself creating insides on the outside, all the while envying beavers, their indifference, their ability to trade inside for outside and back again, without suffering. It's different, when you can leave, when you want to, not just physically. The Board, Garbage Bin left the orphanage, but never really left, died because of it. I'm not sure I really left, the hospital, stopped being a client. I'm trying, just not there yet. Maybe will never get there, will become my father. The people in the SUV, probably people who lived there, in the neighbourhood, probably forgot something, at home. They noticed the line, of course, the line of evacuation, the line they were questioned at, by the police. They noticed it without caring, all that much. They had never felt trapped in it.

At the zoo, local birds, free, would hang around, hoping to be fed. When food was scarce, especially. The records, scanned, recognized, corrected, didn't name the species, just commented on the fact, its effect on caged animals. The escaped cockatoos always came back, for food. An otter escaped once, they found it at a fish market. It was when my father was on the street, struggling, that he got himself readmitted, at the hospital. Basic needs, basic drives. Seeing walls, cages, here, the desire by people not driven by basic needs, to live inside them, I don't really understand it. I don't understand Oksana's parents, who could have left, were ordered to leave, putting themselves in danger, by staying in their cage. A nice cage, before it burned, but still. Maybe that's a condition, needing to be managed. A condition that might have caused their death, if not for the miracle, of their daughter. Yet they thrived, in the city, in this world, on the outside. They were, are parents, they have the distillery, a successful business. A more successful business, it seems, than those of the people in the ring, the ones who talked to me, in the bunkers. I know nothing more, about them, their situation. They just don't seem like The Board, Garbage Bin. They could have died, have tics, urges, manias. They can still communicate, interact, outside. They have succeeded, I guess, where I will always struggle. I've shifted, my writing, in this notebook. It has left Ham behind, jumped to the present. Perhaps I shouldn't, not very organized. Oksana is at the desk, talking to a nurse, the first time I've seen her, since all this started. She's alone, surrounded by people. Just no one who could be her father, mother. She looks worn, tired. Everyone looks that way, in the room, waiting. Each expresses it differently, I'm sure. If Ham were here, he'd point that out, describe it, using better words. For Oksana, I would say pale, not chalky, but a white greyed with time, scraped by stretchers, wheelchairs, all manner of things for the sick and damaged. Her fatigue reflects the hospital, blends with it. Things happened, between Vista Verde and the hospital. Ham's not here because he couldn't film in the hospital, security told him so. And he couldn't wait, not filming, because he's Ham. So he left, leaving me, who could wait, write, without conflict. Oksana knows I'm here. She's done with the formalities, with hospital staff. She sees me, is walking over.

Fuck, I need a drink. They came out more as a sigh than a statement, Oksana's words. I nodded, got up. At the door, before passing into the orange-brown wall of smoke, I fished a mask out of my bag, for her. We left the hospital, together, masked. Saint Luke's, the hospital, the same one where I ended up, as a patient, after the incident, at the archives. I wasn't sure at first, I am now. It doesn't matter, it never matters. For me, hospitals are split into two, those for patients, those for clients. After that, they are institutions, in-terchangeable. Except Saint Anne's, where people are just sorted, sent elsewhere. The doctors, at the hospital, where I was a client, had the same idea. They always tried to steer us to some sort of institution, when we left the hospital. A stable, routine environ-ment. Medical institutions, hospitals, where they could handle a relapse, were preferred. Never mattered which, so long as there was a need for orderlies, janitors. I landed at the archives instead, that time, but ended up in a hospital, anyway. Waiting for Oksa-na, writing, it was the first time, for me, for both waiting, writing, in a hospital, for patients. The people, around me, waiting, in the room, seemed normal, largely normal. They understood bound-aries, imaginary lines, socially constructed. They would have un-derstood the river valley, before the break was cleared, the city, despite the spread of buildings, factories into the ring. What the lines really meant, all the details, they wouldn't have known. Also normal. So, I was able to write in peace, relative peace. Cough-ing, talking, announcements, a hundred other noises, overlapping, conflicting, filled the room. Writing, in the notebook, created its own sort of wall, against distractions, those sorts of distractions. In the hospital, where I was a client, many others had conditions making those boundaries, imaginary lines, socially constructed, invisible. I needed the blue-grey wall, a solid wall despite its misty air, to write. In some ways, the outside, even in a hospital, is easier. That said, now, writing in my writing room, in the house, is easi-est. The door is usually open, but I can close it, when I want. No cameras, security, police, imposing a presence of order. The walls are a clean white, though I've been here, in this room, for a couple of months, though the orange-brown haze has spread, beyond the city.

I felt like a duckling, following whatever happened to be in front of it, whatever might be its mother, switching from Ham to

Oksana, in the smoke of the city. It passed, I don't have a mother, never did. Something that never was can't be replaced. I just wanted to interact with Oksana, Soupy, Ham. Not very good at it, I guess, but maybe good enough. Can't hope I'll get better, too old for that. Can still hope to manage my condition, myself, better. Practise the life skills, taught at the hospital, where I was a client. Under the fluorescent lights of the hospital, where I was waiting, writing, I didn't notice the hazy twilight darken, into night. Outside was actually brighter than during the day, lights on the ground had multiplied, though everything was still unfocused, dull. I thought we were going to the metro station, home. It was a long day. Oksana really wanted a drink, apparently. We went to a bar, black, white, red. Black and white tiled floor, ceiling, mix of black, white objects on the black walls, red booths, tables, lights. Not all lights were red, just enough to pinken the white, Oksana's skin included. So, black, pink, red, I guess. Oksana ordered, a whiskey sour. I went with a gin and tonic. It didn't glow. Oksana leaned back, sighed. The music covered the sound. There was music, there's always music, I don't usually write that. But it covered the sound of Oksana's sigh, so I'm mentioning it, now. Another aspect of life, not one included in the life skills, taught at the hospital, where I was a client. Another aspect of life I don't really understand. I expected her to talk about her parents, the source of her fatigue, why she was at the hospital. I thought it'd be like the cop, with the single job, don't let anyone unauthorized past the barrier. His rant, against her parents, staying in their gilded cage, risking death. Instead, she brought up George, the house, me. The house had been filled with actors, at first, who played small parts, in the city. Lots of small parts, lots of productions. Not just on stages, on the screen, too. Owned by theatres, studios, rent deducted from the pay, of residents. The stable, they called it. Not the only one, apparently. George was an actor, resident, for years.

Times changed, as they do. Stables weren't a thing anymore, not ones owned by theatres, studios. George was tired, of his small parts, always small parts, managed to get some money together, bought the house. Not many actors stayed, after that. Servers, factory workers, artists, students, an unpredictable mix. The house was always full, anyway. George never advertised, word of mouth sufficed. He kept the house up, cooked, was content, no longer chasing a couple of lines a night. A second whiskey sour followed the first. Then the question, how I ended up there, in the house. Me, isolated from the world, a client in a hospital, walls all around me. George had said a little, just enough to avoid conflict, later on. He wouldn't say more, preferred that residents talk, among themselves. I had no answer, played with my lime wedge, brown in the red light. I don't know, I finally said. A keeper, attendant, at the hospital, where I was a client, did something. I didn't say that, about the keeper. Had to be true, I guess. I just didn't pay much attention, not even to Nurse Galverson, who gave me this notebook. Doctor Wimsatt commented on it, in a meeting, ignoring people in the hospital, writing about the zoo. I went where they told me to. They drove me, actually. To the door, to George. A hand off. There might have been paperwork, something saying I arrived undamaged, condition managed. All I remember is writing, in this notebook, in the hallway, on the nightstand. Yet Chac the baboon, the brown hyenas, are still clear, perfectly clear. Then another question, about the hospital, my condition. Not worded like that, the music seemed louder, but about where I was before, if I didn't mind her asking. She would understand, if I didn't want to respond. I didn't want to respond, to the question. I couldn't say nothing, it wasn't like the night of Solomon Nagler, the films, the self-hating Jew. Oksana, Soupy, Ham could talk, the banter, stories could flow, and I could listen. I could be passive. Oksana, perched on the chair, in the hallway, of the house, was an individual. I had to say something then, too. Jacquot, Polly, Polly wanna cracker? Now, she's an individual again. No Soupy, Ham. No parents, just her, pink, under the red lights, across from me.

Life skills, at the hospital, taught to clients. Computer use, cooking, banking, trades, a hundred other things, sex. Not sex as an act, in isolation. Sex, attraction, desire, rejection, domestic life, families. Clients were scared, of women. They had desires, didn't know how to handle them. Sometimes led to violence, tragedy. It was natural, to have the desires, to touch, enjoy another person. A healthy part of life, if done right, if there was consent, adult, meaningful consent. I was looking at Oksana, across from me, the lessons floated around my head. I expected fear, the doctors told me there'd be fear. Desire. The first time on the outside, alone, with a woman. Not completely alone, there were others under the red lights, in the bar. But alone. I felt nervous, increasingly nervous. I wasn't scared, didn't feel desire, just a sort of emptiness, around the wavering flame, in my jack-o-lantern head. And that emptiness wasn't staying empty, it was filling, with anxiety, threatening to drown the little candle, at the centre. If I was normal, human, I'd be feeling these things, the doctors said so. A part of a happy, healthy life, they said. I mean, I didn't feel anything meeting with Doctor Wimsatt, her bottle of gin. She was a doctor, though, no different than Doctor Todd. Oksana's not like that. I was supposed to say something, I couldn't say nothing. I wish she'd just talked about her parents, others, her life. Not me, there was nothing here, nothing behind the façade, nothing human. Human-like, probably less-than, that's all there was. I'd be kicked out of the house, my writing room, where I'm writing now. George would realize his mistake. I wasn't good enough, to play even the smallest part, read a single line. Over twenty years, doctors waffled, over my father's condition, whether it even was. The judgment of Doctor Wimsatt, her bottle of gin, wasn't any better. How could I think it was, why trust it more than Doctor Todd, his misshapen skulls, who sent me to the archives. I was feeling something, sure. My condition, my grip slipping.

Giraffes. Desperation led to giraffes. I said it out loud, the word. Giraffes. On a safari, in Africa, collectors were looking for giraffes, for the zoo. The national zoo, when it first opened. Oksana was looking at me, a weird expression, on her pink face. I thought it was weird, squinty eyes, askew. A giraffe was captured, I continued. They were fragile animals, though, are fragile animals. A newspaper got wind of the news, of a new giraffe captured for the zoo, decided to run a contest, for kids, in local schools, to name it. The collectors were worried, because giraffes were fragile. They had one, captured, alive, but there was a good chance it would die, before reaching its destination. His destination. He was a boy giraffe, the newspaper wanted confirmation on that, for the contest. The locals called him Mfaume, princely emissary. Soon after, still in Africa, he collapsed, died. Acute pneumonia. Exactly why the collectors were worried, that the kids would name, get attached to, an animal already dead, or soon to be. Traumatic, for the kids. But they found two more, held by the game department, in the Sudan. They were put in crates, in a coal bunker, on the ship across the sea, laid down during strong weather, so they wouldn't break their necks, legs. Nobody was confident, that they'd make the journey, alive. A message was sent only a day out, so the zoo would be prepared. The contest had gone on, a name chosen. But with a second giraffe, a girl giraffe, a second contest had to happen, at the last minute. The two arrived alive, to celebration and record numbers of visitors. The names chosen, Hi-Boy for the boy, Dot for the girl. The man who ran the contests, for the newspaper, was exhausted, relieved beyond words there wasn't a third. Oksana's expression had changed through the story. Horror, at the sudden death, discomfort at the conditions of the crossing, amusement at the names.

At least, that's what I understood, I don't generally understand much. The server came, I ordered a whiskey sour. Gin and tonics didn't make much sense, if they didn't glow.

I played Jacquot, repeating a story. It made my life easier, being human-like. Oksana was distracted, seemed amused. She didn't want to talk about her parents, their gilded cage. I didn't want to talk about me, the emptiness of me, having missed out on life, outside. I had to be what I was not, to make it, outside, too old to adapt, change. But I couldn't manage it, being the person the doctors told me I needed to be, interacting the way they taught us, to interact. At least not then, not now, as I write this. Odd animal stories, names, from the zoo weren't enough, aren't enough. But they were, for that moment, to distract me, to distract her, from what we couldn't deal with. Oksana may not have a condition, not like me, but her parents also needed to be managed. At the hospital, as a client, I always thought of mothers, sisters, the vague shapes in the mist of the blue-grey wall, the receivers, senders of letters, the occasional visitors, once or twice a year. Daughters never occurred to me, I guess because clients don't have a lot of kids, aren't much for parenting. You have a thing for funny animal names, Oksana observed. I shrugged. Any more? I told her about Guy Fawkes, the hippo cow. And Jumbo, Jumbina. Elephants. Jumbo wasn't the famous one, the one giant even for an elephant, part of the circus, run over by a freight train, in Canada. Probably not run over, too big. Killed, anyway. The zoo Jumbo was just named the same because the name was famous. Jumbina required no explanation. I was sure then, Oksana was amused, laughed, shook her head in disbelief. The hospital, where her parents were, seemed to recede, take its place among everything else in her busy life. And then we left, the bar, the red lights, for the orange-brown haze. Unmasked, we walked to the metro station, followed the fluorescent lines, to the train, the suburbs, home.

Two security guards, at the bunker entrances. An announcement, by the minister, waving duties, for some things, in the annexation area, for five years. Fewer people, delegations, are coming, but not that much fewer. I wondered if words written, on protest signs, replaced those spoken to me. I wondered if the announcement was a result of bunker input, the movement, or something else. Nothing was connected, in a clear way. Not that it should be, for a Clerk I, Special Opportunity Class. I guess part of understanding better, on the outside, is knowing what I shouldn't even try to understand. Today, a delegation of aggregate extractors, companies that mine gravel, was the highlight, which is to say different, for me. I didn't know, before, that companies mined rocks, mined anything, in the ring. Raw materials usually came to the suburbs, by rail, water, from the countryside. Then they were turned into something else, to be sold, used in the city, or elsewhere, but largely in the city. Rocks, maybe that's the next change, in the movement, the next generation, of violence. There was no sign of it, that I could see. That doesn't mean it wasn't already happening, some sort of violence, with rocks. Life moved on, had to move on, like Lucien, others, at the archives, ministry. Working, protected from the orange-brown smoke, in buildings. There was a moment when I was free, to look for Oksana, Soupy, Ham, find them divided, understand them, Oksana, Ham, a bit better, as individuals. Not too different than taking the bus to the river valley, when it was green, alive. Moments escaping from repetition, in context. But I still need the repetition, to manage my condition, the work, for money, to live. Work's normal, helps me be normal.

Bags of clothes, along the wall, labelled, pants, shirts, coats. I was at a table, to the side, by the bags, listening to those who wanted to talk, reading scribbled notes. I was distracted, thinking. Didn't really need to think, to write, typing, on the computer. Why I can do it, without issue, day after day. I can think, usually, but sometimes, my condition leads me astray. Not too far, I'm good at managing my condition. Just far enough, to not be able to process, work. If I needed to think all the time, I'd fail. I'd risk having to go back, to the hospital, as a client. Police, the person sitting in front of me said. A word repeated that day, in context. And other days, but that day it registered, beside the bags, of second-hand clothes, for the less fortunate. Like me, if I became my father, ended up on the street, had to beg, to come back, inside. Before the but, the persistent but, was talk of security, support for the project because then the suburbs would have police, a municipal police force. Instead of just sheriffs, deputies, who struggled to handle urban problems. The city had already spread, beyond the boundaries of the city. They needed something more, to mark the presence of order. It was the first change, in the bunkers, that seemed linked to the movement, the orange-brown haze, covering the ring. The few times I'd been to the city, I saw police cars, crawling along, marking the presence of order. Never seen sheriff cars do that. It made sense, I guess. It's just nobody had thought about it, as an issue, to bring up with me, before the disorder, visible disorder. Most still didn't want the project to go through, as it was, even with the five years relief. Police were important, now. Economic survival was more so, and five years was nothing. 25 years, maybe. I was distracted, because I read Annie Ernaux. Happening, Cleaned Out, A Woman's Story, others. I do still read, these days. It's easier, now, to read. Nobody rips out the pages, before I can get anywhere, understand the story. Susan Buck is gone, doesn't send me books, but so are the older boys, men who forced me to do things. They're still valuable, books, even without the older boys, men taking them, destroying them. I'm still anxious, around books, a little anxious, that I'll do something, hurt them. I don't keep them, don't own them, too much responsibility. I borrow them, read them, all the way through. Don't understand them, not completely. Maybe had I been able to, to read them, all the way through, when I was a boy, I'd be better at it, now, here. It's too late, I'm too old to change. Ernaux is harder, than most. She writes about life, her life, a life lived. She wrote that she wrote her romantic adventures and lived her books, in a circle, incessant. Like the quote above, noted by Nurse Galverson, I guess, about her life and writing being linked, in a complicated way. It didn't seem normal, doesn't seem normal. But maybe I'm doing it, sort of the same thing. Incapable of living, on the outside, I'm living here, on these pages, in this notebook. A story marked not by safaris, double boiler hats, but the records of the zoo, written, that I scanned, recognized, corrected. A half Ernaux, at most, as she has a life, has had adventures. She had parents, to love, to hate, when she was a girl, an adult. I have repetition, in context, in the hospital, as a client, on the outside. Life skills in place of a life.

Something to think through, as far as I can. Writing, life. I wasn't distracted by that, in the bunker, beside the bags, clothes. I don't understand much. It still seemed clear the happening in Happening was an abortion, illegal, bloody, difficult, absurd. I wondered, why Nurse Galverson wrote the quote here, in this notebook, under sins. That could be the answer, a happening. Seems wrong to follow that with what I have been writing, what I'm writing now, not really getting sins, confessions, priests. It just seems serious, important, real, nothing like panicking in an empty square, before city hall, over nothing. Ernaux thought like Doctor Wimsatt, that sacrifices, sins, two simple columns, did not lead to truth, order. The fancy Catholic school, confession, priest, stood in the way of working through thoughts, feelings. Nurse Galverson was taught ending a pregnancy was a sin, I guess. Just don't know if she wrote it here because she believed it, or because it was what the priest expected. Or she just liked the thought, of a body, sensations, thoughts becoming writing, dissolving in the head and the life of others. The doctors didn't cover abortions, among the life skills, taught at the hospital, to clients. Not really relevant, apparently. Had I paid more attention, at the hospital, to Nurse Galverson, I don't think I'd have learned about her life, the rest of her life, outside. Don't know why Susan Buck sent me books, by Ernaux, among others, many others. But still, Ernaux. I was supposed to learn something, I guess, unless they were just books she had, read, didn't want to keep. I don't think I can think through it. It's just more life I've never had, never will. I couldn't, is the only difference. Not something I missed out on, not like the games I never learned, whose lines cover the floors, of gyms. Ernaux had her abortion, after searching blindly for someone to help. The procedure done, the foetus was supposed to come out, in time. It did, with complications, almost killed her. She found herself in a hospital, as a patient. Everyone was rude, disdainful. At first, she thought it was just her, after what she had done. But she was a student, at the university, which was something. She wasn't The Board, Garbage Bin, she could interact, communicate. Her treatment improved. She came across a teenager, poor, pregnant, in the ward. Who was treated worse, from beginning to end. It wasn't the abortion, Ernaux wrote, but the condition, of being poor, pregnant, powerless. That girl, in the background, the one not writing, was my mother. Not the specific girl, at the hospital, with Ernaux. The generic girl, not even a Jacquot, able to imitate, repeat. Voiceless. No blame, anger. At my mother, for not being my mother. No point. Could have been the reason, Susan Buck sent me the books. Understand better, why I was abandoned, to the institution. Thinking it through, it doesn't make sense. I'm thinking about Ernaux, her experience, because of Nurse Galverson, this notebook. Susan Buck never singled it out, underlined it. One book, among many. And she was direct, in her letters. A beer, beside the notebook, Oksana, Soupy, Ham, in my writing room, lingering, leaning. I'm going to stop, writing. Interact.

Births were important, in the zoo. Molly, a common European brown bear, was singled out, in the records. Every two years, cubs were born, for 16 years. The first year, one cub, female. Two years after, three, stillborn. After that, three live cubs, every time. Impressive, important, popular. Lots of specimens, for cages. And bear cubs attract visitors, cute and playful. Patients, after the hospital had inmates, before it had clients, were pushed outside, those with marginal, manageable conditions. Not many supports, almost all of them failed. Opportunities were limited, not all permanent. One opportunity, harvest, picking fruit. My father picked fruit, in the countryside. My mother, a girl from a local village, also picked fruit. Every hand, not occupied by something more important, picked fruit. They had sex. Harvest finished, my father went back, to the hospital, as a patient. My mother was the shame of the village, disowned by her family. Her mother sent a note, to social services, saying the family couldn't handle her. A social worker investigated, a judge decided, to lock her up. In a home, for unwed pregnant girls. Susan Buck was the social worker. Girls learned life skills, weren't going to be in the home forever. Babies were had, on the inside, hidden from the world. Mothers were sent out after, but not as mothers, unless their families wanted them back, or they could get married. Too hard, on the outside, as a single mother. My mother couldn't be my mother. It would never have worked. She did get married, apparently, had other kids to mother. On that, Susan Buck was not direct. I think I understood, it seemed clear, at the time, when I read the letter. In the end, I was my father's son. Predisposed. My foster mother wrote to the authorities, told them I was a burden. I was acting out, having episodes. Maybe it was epilepsy, they didn't know. It was just too much, I guess. I don't blame them. The note was given to the hospital. I was picked up, passed through Saint Anne's, sorted and sent on. The sorting included a family history, the doctors read my father's file, saw similarities, in our conditions, concluded that I was very much his son. I learned later, about his condition, over twenty years, of contradictions in how the doctors saw it. Didn't matter. Maybe if my mother, the girl who gave birth to me, wasn't so poor, didn't have instinctive perversions leading to casual sex, I would have something better in me. But I existed, because my parents were weak, perverse, sinful. My mother was young, was able to get better, leave her condition behind her. I was young, too, once. Just never got better, only older.

My interaction wasn't interactive. My back wasn't to Oksana, Soupy, Ham, my nose not in the notebook, an improvement. More human, I guess. I also looked at the bottle, really looked at it. It didn't have a label, I didn't learn much. Oksana, Soupy, Ham were actually talking, in the writing room, where I wasn't writing. You know I've been looking for a name for my new distillery, Oksana was saying. Your science lab? Soupy asked. Doctor Ethanol's something something, Ham said. I'm thinking The Great Jumbina, Oksana continued, without distillery or spirits or anything like that in it. The focus is gin, so it'll be The Great Jumbina Gin, for the most part. What do you think? Any way to put juniper in there anywhere? Soupy asked. Jumping Jumbina Gin, Ham suggested, pure class. Oozing out its boozy pores, Soupy added. An elephant with a juniper sprig in her trunk, Oksana continued, done as a coat of arms, for the visual. I lied, I did say something. Dot Distillery, Great Jumbina Gin, Guy Fawkes Firewater. Oksana explained, after that, to Soupy, Ham, the zoo animal connection, my stories. She wasn't in theatre, apparently. She had followed her parents, into liquids culture. Yet she was here, in the house, in the ring. It wasn't that different than theatre, with the smaller stages, newer playwrights outside the city, the more established within. I was amazed, not that she followed her parents, in some ways, just that she remembered, the stories, especially since she hadn't turned them into words, on a page. They were a distraction, from my condition, her parents. Now, they could be something more, different. Yet I was still Jacquot, echoing what was scanned, recognized, corrected. The stories had a life, beyond me, after me. The point of the digitizing project, I guess, at the archives, to give the records new life. I hadn't changed, wasn't supposed to change, was too old to change. Human-like is, for the moment, enough. Regardless, it strikes me, writing this, that the relation between liquids culture and the liquids market must be complicated.

Film night, at the house. It wasn't the first film night, apparently. I just hadn't ever paid attention, avoided the common room, like at the hospital, where I was a client. Ham mentioned it, then mentioned it again, and again. Another form or repetition, in context. He had put together what he captured, when we were together, in the city, behind masks, in the orange-brown haze. A Self-Hating Jew production? Soupy asked, plopping down on a sofa, bowl of popcorn in hand. No, Ham responded, that's the Judean People's Front. We're the People's Front of Judea! Judean People's Front. Cawk. Right, Soupy said, we don't hate ourselves, we hate the Romans. The only people we hate more than the Romans are the fucking Judean People's Front, Ham replied. Enough with the Monty Python, George cut in, on with the entertainment. No offence to Ham, Oksana pointed out, but Monty Python's probably more entertaining than his movie. None taken, Ham said, more educational, too. With that, he pressed play. I was back in the world of a couple of weeks ago, only not. It was straightforward, as Ham had promised. Just the footage taken that day, cut together to contrast movements, I guess. I wasn't sure, there was something going on with colours, changing, patterns, moving. It seemed there was a reason for it all, some logic. That it escaped me was not surprising, to me. It was grainy, as promised, but not intentionally so, not like Nagler, more an ordinary result from the interaction, between lens, smoke. There was no sense of inside, outside. The film cut between opposite sides of walls, fences, lines, chasing something else. That, I could grasp. There isn't much point in writing more about it, here, in the notebook. It'll be the same as what I wrote, in the hospital, waiting, just after we lived it. Only out of order. Or, in another order, maybe a better order. No point of writing about it, except for one more thing. Susan Buck. Ham did capture the waiting room, at the hospital, for a while, before he was asked to stop, by security. And he captured Susan Buck, at the desk, talking to staff, in the same spot as Oksana, sometime later. She looked like her, more like her than how she looked in the restaurant, under the dim light. When she came to visit me, at the hospital, where I would later be a client, she looked like this. It was the context, bright fluorescent lights, light-coloured walls, that made her who she was, for me. It was more, of course, the provider of books, the sender, receiver of letters, but in a way that made it clear, she was not a mother, sister, not to me. The image on the screen, skipped to another moment, another place, and then another. My mind stayed fixed, on Susan Buck. It wasn't in that instant, captured, but I saw an advocate for someone, voiceless, making things happen, in the hospital. An advocate who hadn't given up on that someone, Susan Buck as she was before she gave up on me. No blame, anger. No point. I closed the door, to my writing room, before writing, in the notebook. Don't know if it's because of the time, spent in the common room, with people, or Susan Buck, or both. I am here, that's all that matters now. Doctor Wimsatt, her bottle of gin, didn't give up on me. I still have my job, with the ministry, the magnetic name tags. My situation isn't perfect, but I'm not my father.

Today, a delegation from the chemical depot, at the bunker. I gathered from the magnetic name tags that, if the people throwing Molotov cocktails got their hands on what's at the depot, it would be a catastrophe, of biblical proportions. I know about the Bible, the Torah, other holy books. Never read any, Susan Buck never sent any. From what I understand, which is never very much, it wouldn't be very helpful, to read them. People usually quote without reading, apparently, without context. It's the references that seem to matter, on the outside, not the story, as a whole. Now I am become Death, the destroyer of worlds. From Hindu tradition, I guess. I remember the line, from the history of World War 2. Repeated a lot. The context was the nuclear bomb, not the book, the sacred text. At least that's how it was taught, in the hospital. Add chemical to anything, it becomes concerning. Chemical spill, chemical fire, chemical wash. I imagine the security at the depot is pretty good, even without city police in the ring. It was a delegation, they sat, talked with the magnetic name tags. I was thinking about rhinos, at my table, off to the side, by nothing in particular. It was a hall, everything to be stored, was stored in another room, off to the side. A usual tactic, collecting animals, on safari, was to kill the mother, capture the young. For a lot of animals, like the rhino, that went without saying. I mean, the act was recorded, the death, the capture, but the why was assumed, accepted. Perfectly functional family units, as far as that's possible, in the animal world, destroyed, for specimens, for the zoo. One time, the collectors, hunters, saw two rhinos, mother and child. They wanted a rhino, for the zoo. They shot the mother, killed her. Then got closer, saw the father. They weren't expecting a father, there wasn't usually a father. They were forced to retreat, to escape violence, death. The mtoto was not captured, that day. Its mother stayed dead. A story not often repeated, in the records, the unexpected fatherly presence. Like at the hospital, the collectors favoured the young. Easier to move, crate, adapt to a new life. More years left in that life, if all went well. All told, the better investment. Disposing of the mother was just part of the process. It's not always the case, though. Sometimes it's the young that has to be disposed of, for the mother to adapt, to a new life. Human babies wouldn't be killed, to be clear. Just put into foster care, put up for adoption. I wondered how many mother-child pairs Susan Buck had broken apart. I wonder how the other kids adapted, how many ended up like The Board, Garbage Bin, me. Kids are good at adapting, it's just that not all of them do. And sometimes, even if they do, it's to the institution, not the outside.

I went back to the hospital, where I was waiting, writing. Multiple buildings mashed together, all hard, sharp concrete, on the outside. Mountainous. No grounds, no enclosure, a couple of trees, alive but not happy, healthy. Maybe it makes sense, to have unhealthy trees, at the hospital. Might give the wrong impression for the humans, though. The haze, dissipated, Oksana's parents, released, I was there, outside, without mask, goggles, just looking, staring at the entrance to the room, where I waited, wrote. Standing, the couple of benches were full of smokers, surrounded by their own haze. Doctor Wimsatt told me to be honest, in this notebook, told me to write about her bottle of gin, so she couldn't use my words, against me. No doctors, no priests, I'm supposed to be writing to work through my thoughts, feelings. It isn't the point of my life, to become writing, not like Annie Ernaux, just help me, manage my condition, live on the outside, not become my father. I needed a destination, is what I told myself. To get out, of the inside I was creating, on the outside, I needed to get out, physically, and a destination gave me a reason, to go. My own version of running water, mud, sticks. The river, the park, even the canal, the square before city hall. The hospital was like that, I said. I knew I was lying, to myself, but that didn't stop me. I'm not supposed to lie to myself here, not if I know it's not true. Even if I don't know all that much, understand all that much. The hospital wasn't the destination, not directly. Susan Buck was. After the restaurant, I was okay. She was there, but she wasn't her, the Susan Buck from my memory. In the middle of all the rest, Oksana, Soupy, Ham, Solomon Nagler, she just sort of got lost. She wasn't important, not anymore. She is one reason why I can write, in this notebook, but all that, the skills learned, are part of the past. Maybe there was something about how Ham's phone, hardly visible with all the accessories attached to it, captured her, in the hospital, that made things different. It was already different, she already looked more like the Susan Buck I knew, under the bright institutional lights, but there was maybe something more. Something I don't understand, can't put into words, something that can only be captured by a camera, by Ham. Whatever it was wasn't enough. I went to the hospital, because it wasn't enough, to see her on the screen. I had to see her in person. Which I didn't, see her in person, not when I was at the hospital, outside, by the sickly trees, not when I was in the room, waiting, writing. To get out, I need more than a destination, if I don't want things to go wrong. I need to plan, organize. I know that. Yet it all slipped away, I went to the hospital without a plan, with no organization. I stood there, by the sickly trees, looking through the glass sliding doors, into the room, at the desk, as if she would just be there, as she was, on the screen. In front of this giant mountain of concrete, hard, sharp, with countless sections, wings, doors. It didn't make sense, for me to be there, by the sickly trees. It's like there was no thoughts to work through, no feelings, just a tic, urge, mania.

Here, in my writing room, writing, I tell myself that I had a good reason, to be there. If only Susan Buck could see me, on the outside, managing my condition, she would admit she was wrong, to have given up, on me. Too late for me perhaps, but for the next little boy, acting out, hysterical crises, not knowing any better. They could still get better, get over their condition, not have to manage it for the rest of their lives, not have to live with the fear, anxiety, of failing, on the outside, of becoming my father, people like him, dead at 32, in the hospital. The collectors, hunters, trappers on safari, for the zoo, had a specific aim. Capture animals easy to move, crate, adapt to a new life. Telling them what they were doing was wrong, would have changed nothing. As useful as my father's plea to the director, to be let out. Susan Buck was my mother's social worker, not mine. I was less important to her than I was to Doctor Wimsatt, her bottle of gin, Doctor Todd, his misshapen skulls. I was only one client, of many, kept more in a file than in mind. Still, I was their client. If my mother succeeded, on the outside, in life, Susan Buck succeeded. What happened to me didn't matter. I could be thrown away, put down. Or, at least, the human equivalent. After the first steps of the separation, it was up to the foster family, then the doctors, to deal with me, decide what to do with me, my condition. I guess I don't understand the books, the letters, why she was even around, years later, to give up on me. I wasn't thinking, when I went to the hospital, stood beside the sickly trees. If I was thinking, capable of interacting, that might be the question, to ask. I don't feel capable, of asking.

Planning, organizing. I have a phone, which is a computer, I guess. Bus schedules. I look up bus schedules. Even when I know the schedule, I look it up. Could have changed, the bus might not come, a delay, a detour, anything. I also look up the weather. Since the man, in the hard hat, vest spoke to Ham about the break, the fire in the river valley, the risk of the wind shifting, changing direction, I look at the wind, its speed, bearing. Before, I just looked at the temperature, chance of rain. In the computer room, at the hospital, where I was a client, the doctors were always troubled, by the internet. It was a life skill, to be able to use it, yet it was also dangerous, made managing conditions more difficult. Use was limited, monitored, supervised. Warnings made it seem like it was the worst part of outside, concentrated. Conflict was everywhere, real, potential, imagined. I preferred the writing room, less chance of conflict. Also didn't use my phone for much, besides bus schedules, weather. Sometimes I get a call, message, from work, one of the ministry people, with a magnetic name tag. From receptionists, reminding me of appointments, with doctors. Susan Buck works at the hospital. I found it, on my phone, on the internet. Director, Client Support Services, Saint Luke's Hospital. Clients, not patients. Seems odd. Don't know if that means the hospital has clients too, if patients become clients, if it's for people like me, to be transferred, as clients, to another hospital. She's no longer a social worker. Maybe directs social workers, who still do what she did. Anyway, I can find her at the hospital. It wasn't a random event, her being there, captured by Ham, his phone hardly visible with all the accessories attached to it. I can find her at the hospital, in the middle of the concrete, hard, sharp, I have the location, of her service. 532, Building B. As if the masses of concrete, added over the years, are still separate, unique. A simple destination, if I wasn't lying to myself before, if the hospital was no different than other places, beyond the house, ministry office, doctors' offices,

pharmacy, library, bank, other stores. But it is different. I'm panicky, just thinking about it. An instinct, like that of an animal in
the face of collectors, hunters, trappers. Only, not all animals are
like that. Rhinos will just blindly charge, straight ahead, myopi-
cally. In season, elk will charge too, with better aim. Wild dogs
will test the situation, more wary than fearful. A thousand different responses, evolved, acquired.

By the next film night, in the city, out of the house, Oksana, Soupy,
Ham had once again become one, in my mind. I had become Jackboot, the name Ham used in the square, before city hall, the day
I went into the city to find them. The smoke was practically gone,
the movement, its offspring, had become normal. It would have
been odd, to not have people protesting the project, in one way or
another. I guess if it had further evolved, used rocks, chemicals,
it would have continued to have an impact. But it didn't. Another film night, it was only the second one, for me. Don't know if
there were others I missed. Still don't really pay attention, avoid
the common room, write in my writing room. I know now, the
beers I drink, in my writing room, are imagined by Oksana. Part
of a culture that has continued. In memory, it makes that first
moment, when she slammed the bottle down, foam spilling over,
declaring culture was cancelled, absurd. Not totally, perhaps. She
supported the cancellation of the season, theatre, gallery exhibitions. She couldn't stop herself from making more, different, liquids, alcohol. I suspect the playwrights still wrote plays, painters
painted. The creations just weren't seen, enjoyed, publicly. Maybe
that's why there was always a bottle, for me. Never asked, haven't
made much progress in interacting, outside. Still, I take Jackboot
as progress. I've moved beyond Lucien, the archives, even if it's
just another name, passively accepted. And not a flattering one,

if I understand the meaning. Ham didn't take the meaning seriously when he used it, the first time. Just the sound, how it felt on the tongue. The others, too. And there's no building beyond the house, made of hard, sharp concrete, filled with people who'd take it differently, expect me to perform. The ministry office, bunkers, are elsewhere. I've managed to interact with Oksana, Soupy, Ham without much interaction. I know the situation won't last, yet I'm content it is, even if just for now. Don't know much about Soupy. For Oksana, Ham, they have enough ideas, energy, creativity to live in the city, to survive if the city swallows them up, along with the rest of the ring. I don't know all that much, just believe it's true.

It was, once again, Ham's choice, which made sense. It was also not his choice, I guess, since we could only go to what was on, in the city. The Brothers Quay. Not as foreign as Solomon Nagler, it still seemed foreign. Polish, if there was a point in common, between the two, it would be Polish sources, language, culture. Not for all the films, not even for most of them. It was still there, what I remember, writing, in my writing room. The most important line from the evening, was in German. Herzensschatzi komm. Sweetheart come, apparently. I didn't know the line, the context, until later. But I knew the context, immediately, watching the film. It wasn't me, a client in a hospital. It was an inmate in an asylum, who wrote those words, endlessly. It was a condition that would never be mistaken, for simulated, hysterical. Not like my father's, mine. It was just a matter of degrees, it seemed to me, watching the film. Watching a woman in a room, writing, in a building looking from the outside remarkably like the ones, at the hospital, where I was a client. Not a plea, like my father. Not whatever it is I write, wrote when Doctor Wimsatt, her bottle of gin, judged my words. Just the two words, over and over. Repetition, in context, just a context more restricted than I have felt, a condition so much more overwhelming. The words, addressed to her someone outside, never sent. A vague understanding, yet piercing, compelling, of the outside, with what, who was outside, the walls. Yet an incapacity, far worse than my own, to interact with it, to survive. It wasn't striking, the condition, in itself. I was close to that condition, in the hospital, as a client. I spent my time, in the writing room, writing, after Nurse Galverson gave me this notebook, with walls, blue-grey walls, between me and that condition, those conditions, conditions of other clients. I knew I was marginal, like my father. I knew I might be able to live, on the outside, not only because I was good at managing my condition, but because my condition wasn't too hard to manage. With the pills, therapy, life skills. No, it was that I recognized it, immediately, how it was captured, by the Brothers Quay, animated. It wasn't like Solomon Nagler, capturing the social, a people. Being Jewish, being Canadian, on the vast prairies. His self-hating Jew was a person, an individual, who killed himself, at 23, but his film was bigger, broader. The Brothers Quay went smaller, so much smaller. The tic, urge, mania of sharpening a pencil, of wearing, breaking the lead, and sharpening again, the accumulation of lines, curves, dots on the paper, shavings on the floor, ever accumulating, always accumulating, impossible to move on, because the situation never improved, can't improve, won't improve.

I went to the hospital again. Different entrance, for Building B, a different layer of concrete in the man-made mountain than where I waited, for Oksana. It was raining, all traces of orange-brown smoke were gone. Trees, flowers, grass blackened had not been removed, replaced. They probably had been, in the square, before city hall, a long time ago. I just hadn't gone back, only know about the ones, between the metro tunnel and the mountain. This entrance had sickly trees, too, maybe slightly less sickly, because of the rain. One smoker sat on the sole bench, under an umbrella, a pocket of light white smoke around her head. I had looked at the weather, on my phone, before leaving the house. I was organized, organized enough to wear a raincoat, a new map in my pocket, stand by an entrance for Building B. I had also looked out the window, before leaving the house. The weather in the city, this part of the city, was not the same as where I was, in the ring. I stood there, outside. I had no plan, no confidence for interacting with Susan Buck, anyone else in Client Support Services. It didn't make sense to go in. It also didn't make sense to stand there, in the rain. Yet there I was.

I don't know anything about asylums for women. When I was an inmate, children and adults were mixed together. Women and men never were. I know even less about asylums in Germany. It still seemed odd, to place her in a room, alone, writing. Unless her family, husband was rich, the institution private. The only rooms where inmates could be alone were isolation cells, later isolation rooms, later reflection rooms. Same room, different name. Having things to write on, with, in the room, was unheard of. Having anything in the room, other than oneself, was unheard of. It was perhaps necessary, to limit the story, to her, her condition. The story of the asylum, would have been of conditions, interacting, without interacting, a mess of overlapping made-up kingdoms. I understood Ham's bringing forward, emphasizing bits of experience, putting them together in a way that added, to the experience. Familiar, so familiar, yet more. It was all consistent, nothing really out of place, just a different place. Solomon Nagler was just foreign, I understood his films as far as I could, which wasn't much at all, just appreciating the textures, the rhythms, the themes clearly spelled out or explained, afterward, by Ham. It was alien, to my experience. The Brothers Quay put in so much, out of place, wrong, alien, and yet it was my experience. Not exactly my experience, I guess, the experience of writing a condition, from inside the condition. Not as a doctor, diagnosing, an audience, observing, the creature in the ring, cage. I was part of the audience, staring, through the screen, into this world, isolated, claustrophobic. I saw myself, madly writing, in a room. I saw myself, perhaps, because it was wrong. There was no exhilaration, just a feeling somewhere between unease and dread. A timeless feeling, just there. The character in the film, after finishing blackening a page, with smudged lines, curves, dots, put the page in the heart of a grandfather clock, where the pendulum should have swung, on a pile of so many pages, so many messages, unsent. Then she moved the hands, with her hand, marking time that wasn't, time without relation to outside, the world, others. Days accumulated, with every page, yet every day was the same. That was comforting for me, my marginal condition. As if what I'm writing here, in this notebook, repeating, could be all there is. Which isn't that bad, for me. Dread, for me, is for time to move forward, for me to get older, worse, become my father. Despite the unease of seeing myself reflected in this tiny world, as grey, grainy, bleak as the reflection might be, it is still not exactly my future. Doctors would never look at her file, to get a sense of what I may become. In Absentia, the title. Another degree of human-like, a stable one.

Those were my thoughts, of the film, itself, knowing a little, no more than that. Then Ham had to ruin it, my illusion. She was a wife, a mother, lost to her family. We were at the same bar, soft blue-white light, dark furniture and walls were still pleasant, even with textures more gloomy, sombre than those of Solomon Nagler. I wasn't really seeing it that way, I don't think. It's just how I remember it. I was fine, comfortably uneasy, comfortably wrong. Soupy didn't ask if the images were too disturbing, this time. I found them more so, just wasn't bothered by it, not yet. My gin and tonic was glowing. Oksana had ordered a gin and tonic. This time I ordered it because I knew it would glow, not because she did. Then Ham talked about her life, Emma Hauck, her children. How she was no longer a mother, not really, because of her condition. I had just looked at her, as an inmate, portrayed perfectly and wrongly. It was a mistake of someone, born into the institution, whose parents were locked away, inside, behind walls, when he was born, whose life couldn't escape that. I knew clients, who came from the outside, became dangerous, to themselves or others. One reason they had mothers, sisters. So many loose analogies, from the zoo, are of collecting, hunting, trapping animals, as so many animals had to come from the wild, at least at the beginning. Shows how little I understand, about life. My life can't be tragic, I don't have enough to lose. Emma Hauck's life was, because she did. I guess that's why the Brothers Quay made the film. I guess that's why the conversation flowed over, around me, in the soft blue light. Oksana, Soupy, Ham filled the air with banter, stories. I was comfortable, still. Nothing around me was hard, sharp. I thought I understood why Doctor Wimsatt kept a bottle of gin in her desk, though was probably wrong. I wanted to dissolve, not in the head and the life of others, just dissolve. There was so little of me, is so little of me. And I know it. I'm not a solitary king, with my made-up kingdom. I'm not even Baron Rothbruce, of Currency Creek. Hysterical simulation is my condition, perhaps some sort of perversion, mixed in. The doctors thought I was like my father, expected me to be like him. And I performed. Through Emma Hauck's condition, a real condition, she was still connected, to her life, on the outside, to her husband, her love, her sweetheart. Her tics, urges, manias, betrayed a substance, something that went beyond, the context, the condition. I had nothing. I absorbed the zoo, the records scanned, recognized, corrected, because there was nothing there, to stop all that from seeping in. I absorbed what the doctors wanted to see, because there was no me, not really. It's the tonic, apparently, quinine, black light, that makes the liquid glow. I learned something else, something new, for me. I'll just never catch up, never have a life to become writing, to lose to madness. The rain, just as soft as the blue light of the bar, falling on us before we found shelter, under the fluorescent lights, of the metro station, strengthened the desire, to melt away. Yet it would have taken more substance, more force, to stop following Oksana, Soupy, Ham.

In Absentia wasn't the only film, just the only film to make me spiral. But I'm good at managing my condition, even if it's make-believe. Especially if it's make-believe. Repetition, in context. Keeps me stable, the house, ministry office, doctors' offices, pharmacy, library, bank, other stores. Life, without literary interest, without adventures, happenings. Not even the quest to find running water, mud, sticks. I mean, I found those things. They'll just never mean to me what they mean, to a beaver.

The project is delayed. The bunkers, public consultation, have reached their limit, my days now go by in the ministry office, in the mall, on the second storey, above the stores, activity. I feel I've made it all the way around the ring, without seeing, experiencing. The animals were put in crates, in coal bunkers, on the ship to the zoo, to protect them from rough seas, wind. My journey wasn't much different. I was told about the basins, factories, liquids market, gravel pits, chemical depots, a thousand other businesses, situations, lives. Or I overheard, the issues, explained to the magnetic name tags, by delegations, in the centre of the room. I deciphered lines, curves, dots, I wrote the eternal but of the project, typed it all out on the computer. Just to be told by the computer I was wrong, didn't know how to write. Sentence fragments, always sentence fragments. The journey around the ring did not lead to an end, a cage at the zoo. I wouldn't call the ministry office a destination, even as a loose analogy. Coming to the bunkers, in person, was not the only way to express the but. Emails, letters, calls. All had to be organized, analyzed. Organizing is a sort of analysis, I guess. For, for with concerns, against, information only. Type of concern. Neighbourhood concerned. Resident, business owner, both, other. I was still writing, deciphering, typing on a computer. In a cubicle, dividers soft, neutral, light brown, almost cream. Magnetic name tags were put away, ties, jackets hung. Surrounding cubicles gave hints of personality, individuality. Family photos, kids' drawings, sports keepsakes, cartoons. The opposite of the hospital, where I was a client. Generally, not absolutely. Some pictures survived, inside, objects, bland, promoting life skills, like this notebook. Anything fun, colourful, unique, did not last. Stolen, destroyed. It was worse, in the asylum, as an inmate. Not much better at the hospital. Individuality was expressed through tics, urges, manias. Projecting outward, the solitary king projecting his made-up kingdom. My chair is complicated now, but comfortable, in this room, within a room. The writing room, computer room, at the hospital, were just rooms, with places, for clients. The archives, too, for clerks. The bunkers were all open, I had my place, at the side. Here, it is more like crates, individual, soft, so we won't hurt ourselves. But not individual, like safari crates. More like the food at the hospital. We aren't exotic, don't need special boxes. Everything is standard, what a human, human-like, needs, to work, survive. No more. The traces of anxiety, that the bus won't come, have passed. My hours are the same, every day. No evenings, no weekends. The repetition, in context, is more fixed. The doctors at the hospital, where I was a client, would be content. Easier to manage a condition here, less chance of failing, having to go back inside. Closer to the ideal, still less than another hospital, with patients. I wondered what beavers would make of the dividers, desks, complicated chairs. Today, I added more rows, to a spreadsheet. Writing, typing, copying, pasting. They would have spent that time eating their way through, beyond, outside. Live for a while, get killed, probably after they had young. Maybe wouldn't make it out of the parking lot, run over, add curves, dots of red to the yellow lines.

Days, weeks pass. I'm writing less, in the notebook. Fewer thoughts, feelings to work through. If I had a doctor, priest, to write for, maybe I'd write more. If outside didn't seem less and less outside, the same issues, duties, taxes repeated, written, typed, in my open-top crate. I tacked a sketch, the label for Great Jumbina Gin, couldn't bring myself to leave it. Took it down, when I left for the day. Then I stopped putting it up. It's in my bag, beside me, in my writing room, while I write. But I'm writing less, in the notebook. I'm staring at the wall, through the wall, into the white cloud. Don't see shapes, vague, out there. I'm already outside, there's nothing beyond this. Yet this isn't outside. The zoo was a loose analogy, humans were to be cared for, released, if possible. Not destined to stay, for the rest of their lives. So long as they weren't a danger, for themselves or others. I've never been outside this long. Except with my foster family, at the beginning. Doesn't really count. I just feel I've switched cages, institutions. I've thought this for a while, since I first started writing, about beavers. I'm good at managing my condition. I'm not good at avoiding the trap, of making the outside an inside. The project is still delayed. The setback has nothing to do with what I've been doing, the words I've been collecting. I've always thought, as a Clerk I, Special Opportunity Class, I wouldn't understand how everything fit together. I still don't understand, not really. But the project is delayed for a feasibility study, for a ring road. The minister decided we couldn't know where to end the city, if we didn't know where the road should go. Apparently, there was a road envisioned, that should go somewhere. It makes sense, to me. A physical line, even a boundary, would make the edge of the city more real, to more people. The city itself would have to respect the line. Or, at least, recognize it. People who talked to me, at the side, in the bunkers, were skeptical. They didn't believe, their words would really be heard, listened to. It was worth coming, saying their piece, to me, just in case. They would have been surprised, if something came of it. The ring road makes me think they were right. Other conversations, other issues, other rooms, are the ones that matter. Writing, typing, copying, pasting, seems more and more like a distraction, in my crate, cage. Like N'Gi's ball, double boiler. It shouldn't matter. I'm making it outside the hospital. I don't want to go back, don't have to go back. A good thing, I guess. It's just that keeping outside outside is hard, maybe beyond me.

I'm writing now. There is something, in my head, another Brothers Quay animation, worth writing:

In the city of cheap human material, no instincts can flourish, no dark and unusual passions can be aroused. The Street of Crocodiles was a concession of our city to modernity and metropolitan corruption. The misfortune of that area is that nothing ever succeeds there, nothing can ever reach a definite conclusion. Obviously, we were unable to afford anything better than a cardboard imitation, a photo-montage cut out from last year's mouldering newspapers.

Bruno Schulz, apparently, wrote it. Ham didn't talk about Schulz, in the bar, with the soft blue light, after the films. Jewish, not self-hating, but dead anyway, shot by an officer, German, during World War 2. Not part of what we learned, about the war, at the hospital, where I was a client. Just the holocaust, in general, which was maybe enough. Too much, for some. Cheap human material. Words I would never have used. Wrong, a familiar wrong, Clerk I, Special Opportunity Class. Cheap human material, sold to the ministry, by the doctors, at the hospital, where I was a client. One less burden, one less idle body, to house, to feed. Broken in the right ways, no perversions, leading to casual sex, leading to another me, to house, to feed. One of the empty headed dolls, childlike, but not children. Just lacking the experiences, to make up a life, a full, human life. The material is there, I guess, just never put together. Or put together askew, warped. Human enough, to survive in minimal human space, to write, type, copy, paste, to interact, minimally. Aware, somewhat. More than Emma Hauck. Able to work through thoughts, feelings, in this notebook, with words. Able to manage my condition, I'm good at managing my condition. With pills, therapy, life skills. Outside is normal, complete. Even an orange-brown world, carpeted with broken glass, seemed normal, in a way. Not normal, in itself, just normal, in context, given the project, the movements for, against. Strong interactions, passionate interactions. I understood, somewhat, understood more, through Ham's phone, hardly visible with all the accessories attached to it. Couldn't handle it all, with my condition. But that's me, not the world. Better to not think, feel, more than I must. I can't remember if I thought, felt as much, before Nurse Galverson gave me this notebook, to write in, in the writing room. I could be a sort of Annie Ernaux, now that I write, in this notebook. Now that my sensations, my thoughts, are becoming writing, I need more life. I can't be Emma Hauck, repeat sweetheart come, timelessly. Not outside. I can't be Jacquot, the bird in the archives, in the middle of the concrete, hard, sharp. I can't keep standing, outside the hospital, by the sickly trees, and the entrance, to Building B. She wrote her romantic adventures, lived her books. I'm aware, I repeat, in context, here, in this notebook. I have no book to live, just my existence, as cheap human material.

It's the city I don't understand. I mean, I don't understand much of anything. But in the context, Brothers Quay, Bruno

Schulz. I feel like I should know, if the city, around which I orbit, has crocodiles, even just a street-full. Zoo records show a lot of crocodiles, donated by families that could no longer handle them. They got them when the animals were young, as pets, captured in the south. They were cute, I guess, playful. Then they grew up. A playful bite was no longer playful. The suburbs didn't have to be a magical ring, just be outside the city, where all sorts of things existed that could not survive anywhere else. A unique habitat, with lots of fragile creatures, impossible to keep alive in the city. It wouldn't take much for the creatures to not live well, around crocodiles. For Bruno Schulz, the concession to modernity, was a street. It seemed like the entire world, animated. A world that should suit me, a cardboard imitation of humanity, where no instincts can flourish, where nothing ever succeeds, whose life skills are drawn from last year's mouldering newspapers. But the crocodiles still bother me.

The mountain of concrete I kept standing in front of may have had crocodiles, sitting on the benches, smoking, passing through the glass sliding doors. Crocodiles were people, a sort of people, with big appetites, few scruples. That's what I decided, what made sense, to me. Wasn't helpful, I couldn't tell them apart, no instincts, apparently. Just instinctive perversions. I didn't think crocodiles were there, at a hospital. More a place for cheap human material, to be repaired, as far as it could be, with needle, thread, patches. Repairs stronger than the original material, risks pulling it apart. I was standing there, again, by the sickly trees, in front of a door, into Building B. It wasn't raining, the plants not sickly, dying were still a rich green. My attention was distracted, by the road, cars, behind me. And I saw Susan Buck, a glimpse, driving by. I'm sure it was her. I wondered how many times, she'd driven by, while I stared at the mountain. I walked around, found a second mountain, of concrete, across a road, connected by walkways, at every level above the ground. I sort of knew it was there, the park-ade, just didn't pay attention. It wasn't the hospital, it wasn't 532, Building B. It didn't occur to me she would be driving. Since I was working, daily, in my open-top crate, at the mall, I took the train, from the mall, to the mountain. Close to the mountain, have to walk a ways. Planned, organized and yet missing so much. Including why I couldn't bring myself to let go. I left the twin mountains, walking in the direction the car had gone, thumb on the new map, in my pocket. It's not as if I thought I would find the car, catch it. It just made more sense, than standing, by the sickly trees. The longer I walked, buildings, houses, shops, people, cars, the more it all just seemed normal. No cardboard, cheap human material, crocodiles. I mean, they could have been everywhere, this could have been the street of metropolitan corruption. Maybe if I had Ham's eye, phone hardly visible with all the accessories attached to it, I would know. It was mongooses, not beavers, escaping their crates, constantly escaping their crates. All crates had footboards, a piece that could be removed, at the bottom. Made sweeping them out easier. Mongooses pulled pins, nails, worked latches, anything to escape. And did the same, to return, for food, be with their mate. If they couldn't get into the bird cages. I'd forgotten. I was walking north, thoughts waffling, between crocodiles, mon-gooses. What I couldn't learn, what I couldn't remember. I wanted to be back in my writing room, writing everything I still had, from the zoo. It didn't make sense. The stories, observations, records weren't mine. They were already stored, digitized, at the archives. I was there, I scanned, recognized, corrected, until I was no lon-ger there. But everything else is still there, the words, numbers, lines, curves, dots. I felt their loss, yet they weren't lost. Refocused on the street, heading north, buildings losing storeys, more lines, curves, dots drawn on them. Repeated, names, words, probably in context, wasn't sure. Maybe they were the context, part of it. More green, flowers, grass, poking up, in unexpected places. Cracks, holes, crumbling concrete, paving, just on the edges, making new edges. The flowers, grass looked healthy, healthier, than the sickly trees, by the mountain, than the blackened ones, at the square, the archives. But there were no trees, not here. No sticks, no running water, just enough mud, under the hard surfaces, for some green to take root. The people, walking by, seemed more willing to show some colour, on the outside, poking through, yet not so much as to become peacocks. If I was paranoid, I would have thought poisonous frogs. The old men, with shopping carts, garbage bags full of cans, seemed more at ease, willing to linger, lean, than in the plaza, square. Staying as their real selves, not just as traces, afterimages. Cheap human material, perhaps, or priceless. Incompatible, maybe, with the market of skills, even at a discount, special opportunity class. If the city has a street of crocodiles, if I somewhat understand the idea, this wasn't it.

Then the colour found a new home, a sign covering a marquee, of a movie theatre. In large, block letters, Performance-ins, Guerilla-symposiums, Culture-wakes. The theatres we went to, Oksana, Soupy, Ham and I, to see Solomon Nagler, Quay Brothers, seemed modest. After the opinions, shared by Isidore Fresne, other theatre managers, in the ring, I expected the city versions to be bigger, richer. Didn't really imagine them, just thought it made sense, with bigger, richer plays to put on, with bigger, richer audiences to play to. Movies, museums, galleries, anything marked as a cultural place, on my map, would be the same, be in the same situation. That's why culture was cancelled, not just theatre. But not all culture, only what was on the map. I just hadn't thought it through. I had thought it was weird, Oksana, Soupy, Ham consuming culture, in the city, not as part of the protests. The culture was foreign, old, as it turned out, Nagler, the Quays. Exempt, I guess, though I hadn't really understood it, found a word to describe it, make it distinct from the rule, of bigger, richer. Bars, restaurants, didn't count at all, though I can't find a reason for it. I just came to believe it. Writing, in this notebook, only goes so far, I guess. Sometimes it just fixes my confusion, my inability to work through, make sense. Bigger, richer was one thing, cancelled culture another, foreign, old yet another. I was mixing them all up. I pulled out the new map, the same as the one left in the cop car, by now just as worn. I looked at where my thumb was. I was not standing in front of a place of culture. My cultural confusion didn't matter. The front could have been a cardboard imitation, a photo-montage cut out from last year's mouldering newspapers. Rich once, dead since. Sockets, for light bulbs, circled everything. Not a single bulb was left. The buildings to either side, were too short, to hide a much smaller building, in behind the wall facing the street. If crocodiles were here, once, they've long since gone. Like animals in the zoo, in the wild, they would need to eat. There hasn't been food here for a while. It's a prop, I guess, what the suburbs would become, if the project went through. What I never understood, actually. The season wasn't cancelled, not really, it just moved to the city, here. For no money. Not visible to anyone, except the sort of people who would talk to me, in a bunker. Looking around, trying to picture a group of magnetic name tags, in this street, I couldn't. Which didn't mean much, doesn't mean much, I guess. Just one more thing I'll probably never understand, how any of this would change, or even stop, the project. The door was open, light, people inside. I don't know if it was because I convinced myself the people inside were like those from the bunker, people I could handle, interact with without really interacting, or because performance-ins, guerilla-symposiums, culture-wakes were connected, in my jack-o-lantern head, to Oksana, Soupy,

Ham. I went in, losing sight of Susan Buck, beavers and all the rest, sheltered from the problems of the outside.

The dead theatre was filled with problems of the outside, just not mine. My skills were of need, by the ministry, because of the project, people's issues with it. The doctors may have found another taker, other special opportunities. The fact is, it was that one, in particular, that allowed me to leave the walls of the hospital, where I was a client. I interacted with nobody, all lingering in the lobby. Their words reached me. I didn't have much context, didn't understand everything. Still, the pause, the ring road seemed to dominate. Speculation about timing, why did the road become an issue now?, ulterior reasons, the road's just an excuse, pessimism, of course the minister is listening to big business, their demand for a new trucking route, and not us. The us was what I didn't really grasp, any more than I understood culture. Vaguely, that is to say. I can say for sure, there was no moping. The lobby walls, ceiling looked freshly painted, orange for the first, black for the second. I felt like a jack-o-lantern in a jack-o-lantern, only they kept the seeds, fertile, in the bigger one. Life, activity, ready to grow, burst out of the theatre, joining the grass, flowers adding colour to the street. Messy, which would be okay. There was no vacuum-thing here to keep things neat, tidy. There was no ticket office, concession, performance posters, a normal context, for a theatre. I wasn't even sure where the actual theatre was. It all made me feel increasingly uneasy, unsure how to act, what to do. I decided to stay, there was nothing sharp, hard there, I wasn't a creature in a ring, cage, everyone in the pumpkin seemed to be a single, potential audience. Normal people feel really isolated apparently, when they're alone, in the middle of a crowd. For me, it's worse when I'm included, when I have to act, meet their expectations, as a human. Oksana, Soupy, Ham are usually different, I'm included without expectations. It's harder when they're split apart. The unease was minor, is what I thought, manageable. I could ignore what I was taught, at the hospital, where I was a client, that I had to interact if I was going to make it, on the outside. Time passed, the conversations swirled, I caught words, phrases, held on to them, contemplated them, let them go. I didn't want to play collector, trapper, hunter. Then a bell rang, startling me. I woman near the back yelled that things were about to begin. Things, the word she used, was not helpful, in understanding, what was going on. The bell rang a second time, echoing off the edges of the room, sinking into the soon-to-be-audience. The group moved, as a herd might, as one, a flourishing of instincts. Nothing like the rigid, formal grouping of magnetic name tags, in the bunkers. They flowed through an orange door, near the back, no different than all the others. I started to wonder if there were dark and unusual passions behind it. I didn't have the same instincts. I wanted to leave, to find myself back in the street, with the grass, flowers poking through. The pumpkin was almost empty, when I forced myself to follow. Oksana, Soupy, Ham were involved in performance-ins, guerilla-symposiums, culture-wakes. I didn't know how, but they were. So it should be okay, what's behind the orange door. I should be okay, my condition should be manageable. Anyway, I repeated, as I do, I'm good at managing my condition.

The theatre was not crowded. Fifty people, maybe. They seemed more in the pumpkin, mixed together, with all the words, floating about. The chair was lumpy, creaky. Not entirely uncomfortable, just odd. Maybe it fit my cheap human material, all askew, warped. We all sat there, an audience formed. Some conversations made it, through the orange door, quieter, sparser. A woman appeared, on the high stage, overlooking the rows of lumpy chairs flat on the floor. Her voice sounded the same as the one announcing things to come, probably the same person. She thanked everyone for coming, claimed the movement was still going strong.

Perhaps a movement, I thought. An offspring of this one, more visible, more active, where the minister would see it, have to react. I didn't know, don't know. Since the rain came, erasing the last traces of orange-brown smoke, putting an end to the life smoldering in the river valley, the situation became hazier. I'm sure there was still something happening, outside dead city theatres, it just didn't have the same impact. The Call of the Wild had been silenced, it seemed to me, from my position, somewhere between the house, ministry office, doctors' offices, pharmacy, library, bank, other stores. And in front of the mountain, beside the sickly trees. At the mountain, it would have probably been drowned out, by the siren call of a life I never had, the life where Susan Buck hadn't given up on me. Where I got better, when I was young enough to get better. In the crumbling street, the pumpkin, Susan Buck, her car, had disappeared, pushed out of my head by other thoughts, captured, released. The woman on the stage, trying to convince the fifty people watching her, listening, that the movement was alive, well, vital to our collective future, brought Susan Buck back. Don't give up on the movement, the woman on stage was saying, without saying it. That's what I heard, understood. A plea, though somehow not a plea as pathetic as my father's. I don't know why. It ended, however, the latest word, on the state of the movement. To make room for an introduction, of the creature, the performance. Doctor Galen Evans, post-doc at the City University, working in the history of ideas research group. Not a stranger to this stage. Going to talk to us about things. The woman didn't know, it wasn't really organized, planned. And then Soupy appeared, on the high stage, overlooking the rows of lumpy chairs flat on the floor. Soupy looked like Soupy, from the house and everywhere else. Even in the ring.

Hello everyone, he opened, a pleasure to see you all here. I've lost track of the number of times I've been up here, on this stage or one of the dozen others set up across the city. I've spoken about cities, politics, suburbs, protest movements and all sorts of other subjects I'm generally aware of and have some background in. Every time, I start by saying I'm not an expert in any of them. Because I'm not. You've all heard this before. If you weren't the converted, you wouldn't be here, honestly. But this warning isn't for you. It's for the people online who might stumble across the video. I've struggled with the whole public intellectual thing, which I have stumbled into through these protests. Easy, accessible, yet counterintuitive ideas dominate the public intellectual field. Well, I have some ideas that I've been throwing out there, but they aren't mine, for the most part, and they aren't necessarily easy, accessible or counterintuitive. More importantly, they aren't conclusive. I've tried to present them in an accessible way, of course, but balance that off the fact that they are not easy or simple. The point, for me, is to highlight their messiness and ambiguity. Historically, movements like this tend to have a purity and purge phase, usually before they collapse in on themselves. Let's avoid all that, shall we? Let's avoid the preaching and true believing. Let's question and learn. I'm not up here because I have all the answers. The doctor simply means I've spent more time than I care to say digging up and working through historical movements, events and theories. None of that will tell us exactly where we should go, how we should act. It will, however, give us perspective and context so we can make better informed decisions. Anyway, that's the spiel, for what it's worth. It's not going to be worth much tonight, as tonight I'm taking a break from all that. One thing that gnaws at me about the whole public intellectual role is the worry what I am saying is not at all relevant and doesn't contribute in any way to public discourse. Tonight I just want to embrace it, irrelevancy in regard to the protests, the movement and the minister's project.

Six months ago, the Pope made a declaration admitting there

was a problem of sexual violence in the Church. It wasn't the usual declaration we've gotten used to hearing over the past several years. It had nothing to do with priests abusing young boys. This declaration was about priests, monks and other men in the Church hierarchy abusing women in the hierarchy, such as nuns. My theory on the declaration is that, after the complete debacle of the Church's response to pedophiles in the ranks, essentially denial and obfuscation, the Pope wanted to take a new approach, admit the problem and get ahead of the scandal. It's hard to say whether it worked, but everything seems to be fairly well contained for the moment. As usual, I didn't come up with the theory that he was getting ahead of the problem in a vacuum. That was the position of a lot of observers at the time. And I remember thinking to myself, in my own nerdy, academic sort of way, that he hadn't actually gotten ahead of anything. Sexual abuse of nuns by men of religious vocations had been a badly kept secret since forever. And by that, I mean since the early days of the Church. Most people didn't know about it because the media and other forms of communication weren't what they are today. The records, among the people who kept those sorts of records, are clear, however. So, good on the Pope for recognizing the problem publicly and doing something about it. Let's just not pretend that it's some great and recent revelation.

Our good friend and Sixteenth Century satirical humanist Henri Estienne wrote about it in his Apologia for Herodotus. In past talks, I've spoken about cities from that time in what is now France, Belgium and Switzerland. Those cities tended to be where the Estienne family moved to avoid persecution. Estienne was a classical scholar and printer who had a giant bone to pick with his so-called peers and society in general. His so-called peers had the affront to translate ancient Greek texts into French not from their original Greek, but from their Latin versions. Because of this, they picked up all the mistakes, inaccuracies and outright lies from the Latin, typically written by Church-associated scholars. That meant that the francophone public interested in Greek ideas was reading contaminated sources. A travesty! It was even worse, though. Francophone society at the time also had it in their collective head that it would be a sin to read about the sinful ideas and lives of the Greeks. Because Greeks weren't Catholic, you see, they had to be immoral. It wasn't heretical, you understand, because the Church didn't exist yet, but it still could lead Sixteenth Century Frenchmen and Frenchwomen astray. It was a bad influence, so needed to be suppressed, except for use by hardy Church-associated scholars.

So, when Estienne put out his translation of Herodotus's works, he started it off with a thorough defense, or apologia, of them. Herodotus was a Greek historian. It's generally accepted that his writing has problems. The role of historian in ancient Greece was somewhat different than that of a modern historian. He didn't exactly support what he wrote with an array of sources, as would be expected now. Beyond that, the Greeks did do things we would find immoral even today, Catholic or not. Pedophilia was not considered a crime, for instance, and cannibalism had its place. Estienne's approach wasn't to prove that Herodotus and ancient Greece weren't immoral, but rather that the Catholic world of Estienne's time, essentially France and Italy, were just as sinful, if not more so. Basically, he aimed to show that the critics were hypocrites. It didn't stop there, though, because critics were shocked, shocked! by the scenes Herodotus described. Estienne needed to not only show the hypocrisy, but set up his own contemporary examples as equally shocking. This pushed his take on society into satire.

What's curious, from my nerdy, academic perspective, is that Estienne didn't present raping nuns in the Church as shocking because of the sexual violence. That was stated as something everyone already knew, or at least suspected. No, to get a reaction he had to go further. He presented it as a question of incest, with everyone in the Church being a family under God. Nuns being sisters and mothers. Monks, priests being brothers, fathers. You get the idea, a whole other level of sin. The Pope, of course, didn't touch on this aspect of the problem in his declaration. So, how far afield was Estienne? I'm just starting to get into the topic, but I can sketch out what I've found thus far and where I think the research is leading me.

Soupy went on, down the path of Catholic incest, I found it harder and harder, to hold onto his words. I suspected other people, in the audience, felt the same way, but didn't know. It was my first time there. I didn't have the benefit, of repetition, in context. It was like the circus animal, in the ring, doing what was natural to it, not in a way that was dangerous, to itself or others, just unrelated to the audience, not meant to entertain. It was sort of entertaining, I guess, in a dark and unusual passions sort of way. The shock value probably helped, especially for those who understood, better than me, the tradition. Someone, in a lumpy chair, suggested Soupy explore incest themes in nunsploitation movies. Another form of culture I know nothing about. Still, it was clear to me that the subject fit better with this notebook, than how I use it. Not that the notebook was meant for it. Not like how kids at a fancy Catholic school would use it, as a guide to life, a clear and proper ledger. Just sins in the sins section. Worth writing, even if it's me, writing, in my writing room, not really understanding all that much. Doctor Soupy. Out of all that, what stuck in my mind was that Soupy was Doctor Soupy. Living in the house, with me, in the suburbs. I already knew, I was the odd one out. Oksana made that clear, when she told me the history of George. Still, Doctor Soupy. Standing on an empty stage, with a microphone, bottle of water.

Painting a picture as puzzling, to me, as Solomon Nagler, Brothers Quay, Ham, with words, history. Only, after, I saw the bare stage, a cluster of people gathered around Soupy, gesturing. No colours, textures trouble my vision, in memory. I wasn't left with a foreign rhythm, focus. It just revealed more of the world, of Nurse Galverson, of happenings, illegal, bloody, difficult, absurd. A world that pushed Henri Estienne, Annie Ernaux to risk death. Receding, I guess, but still with us. So much hasn't changed. Which makes no difference, to me. The outside is just there, normal, however it is. It isn't like the asylum, which became a hospital, where I started as an inmate, became a patient, then a client. I know right from wrong, as a life skill. My instincts have never flourished, I don't think. I see myself, in the wrong, in the Emma Hauck on the screen, with the unmoving clock. I will never succeed, reach a definite conclusion. Regardless of the crocodiles.

I waited, after. Sitting in my lumpy chair, listening to the creaking of all the others, as people got up, most left, to the orange room, perhaps outside, no better prepared to make decisions, about the direction the movement should go. A movement I thought was already dead. Performance-ins, guerilla-symposiums, culture-wakes didn't seem relevant, when everything was on fire, lost in the orange-brown haze. Yet the fires are gone, and the movement continues. Sort of. A small group had stayed, hovered around Soupy, on the high stage, talking, debating, gesturing. I watched, some words escaped, made their way to me. I ignored them, let the activity run its course. Even as a smaller, tighter group, they didn't blend like the magnetic name tags, delegations. And I was there, led by tics, urges, manias I couldn't manage. No better at stopping myself from standing outside the mountain, by the sickly trees, than Emma Hauck could stop herself writing sweetheart come. Yet I was there, in the the dead theatre. I hadn't kept walking, after a car long since gone. I was there, at ease, in the audience, what used to be the audience, in a lumpy chair. Soupy was there, but on the other side, of the line. I hadn't leaned on him, not like Ham, in the square, before city hall, like Oksana, leaving the bar, unmasked. It was a good moment, for me. The group on the stage dispersed, Soupy saw me, approached. He was surprised, to see me. He was going to join Oksana, Ham, some others, at a bar, if I wanted to come. I nodded, cringed at the parrot-like squawk my chair gave, as I got up. He talked to people, lingering, leaning, in the pumpkin. A makeshift bar had appeared, the people there looked serious, sombre, like they were at a culture-wake. Or a wake for the movement, as it had existed, beyond the dead theatre, before the fires.

We went to the bar I had been to with Oksana, where I told stories of giraffes, elephants. Black, white, red. Black and white tiled floor, ceiling, mix of black, white objects on the black walls, red booths, tables, lights. Not all lights were red, just enough to pinken the white. So, black, pink, red, I guess. I couldn't tell if Oksana was as tired as last time, staying with her parents, at the hospital. Her face was just as pink. She, Ham and some others were already at a booth, when we arrived. Wagers on whether they ever ask me to speak again? Soupy asked the table. You did the nun raping talk? Ham asked. As promised and advertised, Soupy replied. Not everyone, at the table, was aware of what was promised, advertised. A long explanation, discussion followed. Everyone agreed the nunsploitation angle was interesting, except me. No instincts, for such things. We should do a marathon at the house, Ham suggested. Don't think George would agree, Oksana replied. A long discussion, about how to put on the marathon, who to invite, followed. Then the banter, stories, ricocheted, off subjects I didn't realize were in the air. I had ordered a new drink, for me, a negroni, focused on that, let the words go by. Nobody wagered, as far as I could tell. Sitting here, writing, in my writing room, I know I wasn't focused on my drink, in the black, pink, red bar. I was focused on Soupy. I was feeling nervous, but didn't know why, not yet. I probably don't understand it now. Now I feel dread, but not about Soupy, not directly. About setting up a meeting, with Susan Buck. I wasn't ignoring the negroni. It just sat there, unless I did something with it. Easier to focus on, than the conversation. This was the second time I was there. I understand Oksana, Soupy, Ham are there regularly. This bar and the one, with soft blue light. Another sort of repetition, dulled by its optional nature, blunted by the alcohol. Doctor Wimsatt only had the alcohol, in her cabin, hidden by the trees. I have nothing, in my open-topped crate.

Soupy. Doctor Soupy. I knew his sort of doctor wasn't the same, as the doctors I see regularly, not like Doctor Todd, Doctor Wimsatt. Yet he might be exactly like them, in a way, in his specialty. He probably aims for conclusive conclusions, to cut through the messiness, ambiguity, digging up, working through. A specialist, but not my specialist, not a specialist of my condition, of cheap human material, the first I think I've met, in my life, in person. One of the reasons the zoo records stuck with me for so long, perhaps. Seeing a world from the eyes of experts, eyes not pointed in my direction. The observations, conclusions could be as accurate as the diagnoses of my father, over twenty years. I wouldn't know. And not where I want to go here. Doctor Soupy, for the world beyond Henri Estienne and whoever else, accepted the messiness, ambiguity. He said so, before he started talking, about raping nuns. Even the nun raping, seemed messy, ambiguous, I guess. Even the happening, which happened, seemed messy, ambiguous, when Annie Ernaux described it, and she was there, without a condition. Without a condition like mine, or worse, Emma Hauk's. She had another sort of condition. I'm getting confused, losing what I'm trying to say. I'm trying to say that Soupy, Doctor Soupy, wouldn't take what I do, don't do, as symptoms of my condition, as evidence supporting a diagnosis. That isn't it either. I mean, George told Oksana, Soupy, Ham things about my condition. That's one of the reasons they accept me, with my difficulties interacting. I wouldn't have been at the bar, black, pink, red with my negroni, not interacting, if they didn't know. They did judge me, had to. Decided I was a harmless weird, not a danger to myself or others. Concluded it, somewhat conclusively. Doctor Soupy, too. Though not as a doctor. Maybe I'm starting to judge what's normal, on the outside. Doctor Soupy, on the high stage, separated from his audience on the floor, in the rows of lumpy chairs. Connected, though, a part of the movement, the original movement, when it was all about performance-ins, guerilla-symposiums, culture-wakes. A part of a conversation, interacting. Then he did something else, he performed, as an exotic animal might, in a circus ring. A doctor, a specialist, no longer observing, researching, but being observed, and not as a specialist, not exactly, just someone who shocks, exhilarates, or causes a feeling somewhere between unease and dread. Shock, unease at nun raping, centuries of it. Shock, unease at a doctor, of history, presenting it as a curiosity. A performance accepted, in the ring, so long as it stays there, inside. Doctor Soupy was no longer with his audience, the movement. Except for me. I had been in the audience, following Ham, his eye, his phone hardly visible with all the accessories attached to it, never feeling close, to what we saw. At ease, being on the other side, no longer in the ring myself, expected to perform. Doctor Soupy was different. The more he pulled away, from his audience, the closer I felt, to him. Another human-like creature, not really normal. Repeating the ideas of Henri Estienne. He wasn't me, with my condition, incapable of interacting. But there was something there, for me. Perhaps that's it, that's the reason, in the bar, black, pink, red, I asked him if he could come with me, to see Susan Buck. It didn't make sense. I needed someone to lean on, someone I had already leaned on, to help me. Not another exotic creature. Even if that exotic creature could function, on the outside, so much better than I. If I'm judging now, do I think Ham, looking at the world through his phone hardly visible with all the accessories attached to it, is normal, on the outside? Oksana, apparently passing her life in a lab for liquids? There is nobody else, in this world full of people. Meeting with my mother's former social worker. A sure sign I couldn't adapt, to the outside, move forward. A sure sign I was too old, my condition too unmanageable, that I needed to be sent back to the hospital, as a client, to die, like my father.

He said yes. Soupy said yes. Didn't even think it through, do his research. The expression on his face, less pink than Oksana's, seemed curious, like the question was curious, though that might've been because I was saying something, period. I don't talk much, I guess. Still, he didn't hesitate, responding. And then my nervousness became panic. I managed to thank him, to get a couple more words out, before shutting down, holding on. Meeting Susan Buck wasn't just meeting Susan Buck, walking up to her and starting to talk. I didn't even know how to meet her, what to do. I couldn't even enter Building B, just stood there, like one more sickly tree. And that was it. My mind was stuck there, looking at the glass door opening, closing, the mountain of sharp, hard concrete around it, everything rose with the light from the bar, bleeding through. Later my brain whirred through possible steps, setting up an appointment, if Susan Buck even took appointments, organizing, planning, talking, interacting. Later. At that moment, Oksana asked me if I was okay, Soupy's expression had changed, from curiosity to worry. I nodded, I managed to nod. An interaction. They didn't insist, just rejoined the flow of banter, left me to deal with what I had to deal with. Which I did. I'm pretty good at managing my condition, especially if it only rises, to the level of a panic attack. It was only then, as the anxiety passed, that I noticed the music. There's always music, but just then, it came to the fore. Typically, it would have been an animal, an anecdote, from the zoo. This time it was different, even with the giraffes, elephants, lingering from my conversation, last time I was there, with Oksana. You see, I've got this disease, I can't shake and am just rattling through life. Lyrics heard, understood. The Modern Leper. Frightened Rabbit. Just looked it up, on my phone. I didn't need to follow through, I thought. Soupy wouldn't care, I was sure he wouldn't. Another imbalance, like my relation with Doctor Wimsatt, her bottle of gin. It's so difficult, for me, to ask for support, it's easy to forget, that others, outside, don't have that problem, not usually. Among friends, and I'm starting to accept we're friends. Only I'm starting to accept, I have to do something about Susan Buck. About myself, actually, in relation to her, who she was.

All it took was an email, sent between filling in two cells, of the spreadsheet, in my open-topped crate. Sent to the general address, Client Support Services, Saint Luke's Hospital. Then waiting a week. I get lots of email, on my computer, at the ministry office. People with personalized boxes here, elsewhere, always finding more notes, opinions, issues, to add the spreadsheet. They also come through interoffice mail, scraps of paper, covered with lines, curves, dots. More of the same, never a definitive conclusion. Except for the meeting, with Susan Buck. Arranged between me, her assistant. Confirmed with Soupy. Like arranging an appointment with one of my doctors, when a standing one won't do. It added a level of nervousness, barely noticeable, always present. It couldn't be overwhelming. The worst thing she could say, was that I was worthless human material, which was clearly not true. Details, she could add painful details, but not many. She was always on the other side of the wall, except for the visits, once or twice a year.

She could confirm I don't have a mother, which I already know. No blame, anger. No point.

I have a new theory, why I asked Soupy to come. With all his research on the sins, violence, committed in convents, other closed institutions, against the small, weak, he wouldn't be so surprised to hear, what happened to me. Or, at least, he'd be better suited, to manage his shock. Which he did. The hospital stopped looking like a hospital, on the fifth floor. We passed giant rooms, filled with open-topped crates, standard human size. Too many windows, cut through the outside walls, to be bunkers. Seemed the right dimensions, though. Far bigger than the ministry office, at the mall. None of the sharp, hard concrete from the outside showed through. This didn't look like the inside of a mountain, a cave for some exotic creatures. It was a controlled inside, designed for endless, indeterminate repetition, in context. For normal people, not just Clerk Is, Special Opportunity Class. Normal people managing clients, files. We found our way to 532, which didn't seem different than 528 to 531. We were received, by a receptionist, who alerted the assistant, who settled us in a boardroom, along the outside wall, windows overlooking sickly trees, smokers on benches, a road, then a whole neighbourhood of houses, buildings. We were early, Susan Buck was late. The chairs were complicated, the room set up with mics, speakers, screens, cameras. Technology to aid interaction. The cameras, mics bothered me. There were cameras all over the hospital, where I was a client, in the bank at the mall, a hundred other places. I just didn't like them there, in that room, at that moment. Then Susan Buck was there, in the room, filling it with energy, warmth. That's the word, perhaps the only word, to describe her. Her eyes, smile, posture, handshake, everything radiated warmth. Something I hadn't felt, in a very long time. The notion, that she could have ever abandoned me, convinced my mother to abandon me, fled my mind in her presence. Introductions were made, with Soupy, an interaction that passed me by. Tomas Stellar, she said, sitting down across from us, you are looking very well. I was crying, I don't know when I started crying, but that's all I had, in response. She continued, her words blurring, but I understood the meanings, generally. It seemed natural, understanding what she was saying, without words. Now, writing, in this notebook, in my writing room, nothing seemed natural. The woman who sent me words. Books, letters. Words I memorized, wrote, sent back to her. More than her presence, it was words that defined us, our connection. Something intelligible and general, yet not writing, I wonder now how Annie Ernaux would have reacted.

Susan Buck was happy I had reached out, was there, with her, in a room, once more. A man now, making his way in the world. She was so proud of me, all I had accomplished. And I was proud, of myself, felt I wasn't in this mountain, but had climbed it. Everything was right, with me, with the world. I had felt I hadn't changed, couldn't change, was too old to change. But none of that was true, I was a success, not as Jacquot, but as Tomas Stellar, a real human being. I was facing in, back to the window, rows of open-topped crates on the other side of the glass wall. Yet I couldn't see past her, her presence. Soupy, sitting beside me, was lost. It wasn't just her who was proud, but all the doctors who had guided me on my path. After my email, she had reached out to Doctor Wimsatt, who had nothing but glowing things to say. Now I wonder what Doctor Wimsatt's bottle of gin had to say. Perhaps it was the gin speaking all along. In the room, there was no gin, no Soko the Chimpanzee-like melancholy. Doctor Wimsatt was perfectly content, in her cabin in the woods. I was her only client, she knew me so well, she didn't even need a file. Words, written, got in the way. They linger when it's best to move along. All the doc-

tors helped me move along, Susan Buck delicately stepped aside
so they could do their work, make me better, help me become the
man I am today. It wasn't without heartache that she exited my
life, but she knew I was in more capable hands. Hands capable of
caring for a child tormented by his demons. The books she had
sent with love, a chaste religious sort of love, only brought me
more torment, attracted more demons. It was easy, in the room, to
see all the older boys, men who ripped up the books, did things, as
demons, my condition, as a demon. Only after, in my writing room,
writing, thinking it through, that I see it didn't make sense. The
others in the cage were just as tormented, as me. Many more so.
The demons, if there were demons, were the people who put us all
in a cage, together. At the zoo, they never did that. Animals were
regularly put in the same cages. If they fought, were incompatible,
they were separated. I don't remember the specific animals, an-
ecdotes, but still. At least children were separated, eventually. No
blame, anger. No point. There were dark clouds, in Susan Buck's
story, of my life. There had to be, to make the present all that much
brighter. She was right, in a way. My life, now, is better. Perhaps
better than it's ever been. If I wanted confirmation, a diagnosis,
there it was. I didn't know what I wanted, exactly. Still don't. I
guess I just wanted to do something, so I would stop standing, by
the sickly trees, in front of the sliding glass door of Building B. It
could have been that simple. She didn't bring up my mothers, biological, foster. Not once. My story, as she painted it, started in
the asylum. It's how I start it, too. I have no parents. I was a man,
apparently, accomplished. Yet I couldn't speak. The tears dried up,
in the warmth. It was still just her speaking. She did pause, once
in a while, to give me, us room to say something. She wasn't trying
to dominate, she just did, by default. Soupy told me he thought she
was saying everything I wanted to know, just with rose-coloured
glasses. He thought it weird there was no mention of my mother,

but it didn't seem like his place to ask, especially if I didn't look concerned about it. I looked happy, apparently, happier than he'd ever seen me. It was so kind of me to come and see her, she continued. I must have such a full, busy life. To take a moment out of it to visit her, someone who played such a small, insignificant role, showed how mature, thoughtful I had become. She imagined I was just as thoughtful, to the doctors, who had done so much more. It became so exaggerated, her manner, yet the sincerity, the spell, held. If there was a witch in this story, it would surely be her. And that was it, the time was up, she had another meeting. Five meetings, probably, back to back. The seed was planted, with me. I was fine, she wasn't important, there was no reason to come back. She didn't hug me. I remember her hugging me, at the asylum. But I was a man now. And she was a stranger.

The spell held until I was back, in my open-topped crate. The email was still there, a single line in a massive column of words, to add to the spreadsheet. Susan Buck was unimportant, now. A rare equal relationship. I would like to have told her, the importance of the books, to me. That I was the man she saw, in front of her, capable of surviving, outside, because of this skill, writing, I never would have had that, without her. I would have liked her to be proud, of something real. But how could I possibly explain that, to a person, who thinks the books attracted demons, torment. Maybe she didn't really think that, just said it. She just seemed so sincere. Regardless, how could I possibly explain that, when I can't utter a single word, when it counts. She never did say exactly what happened to me, at the asylum, with my tormentors. Soupy understood anyway. He understands things better than I do. He wasn't shocked. Or he managed it well. I never got a sense, of what she did now. The more I write, work things through, the more unanswered questions appear. Maybe I could write a message, send it. Thank her, for meeting with me, us. Then ask. But none of that was important, a second email, to be crushed, under the weight of a hundred opinions, to add to the spreadsheet. I had wondered, before, if I could make a difference, for others. If, after seeing who I'd become, she wouldn't make the same choice, abandoning me, convincing my mother to abandon me. She hadn't seen who I'd become, in the room. And who I'd become was incapable of changing that. Who I've become, someone who stares more and more at the cloudy wall, not writing, because those hundred emails give me nothing to work through, not anymore.

The bus was twenty minutes late, this morning, between home, the ministry office, at the mall. My phone told me so, interacting more and more with the world around us. New technology, bus tracking, wasn't there when I left the hospital, stopped being a client, wrote in the bunkers orbiting the city. No place for anxiety, now that my phone knows where the bus is. I went back to the house, for the notebook. I knew I had the time. After the office, I took the metro, followed the fluorescent lines, into the city. The same train that took me to the mountain, to stand by the sickly trees. Only, I didn't. Meeting Susan Buck worked, sort of. It was no longer a tic, urge, mania, going to the mountain. I sort of wish seeing her would have made her fade away, somehow. No reason for it, that I can think of, but there might have been one, one that I just didn't really understand. Her spell faded, the silliness of what she had said became so obvious. I might have been angry, at myself, for not being stronger, in that room. There was no point. I'm not the man she pretended I was, not even the human she might have seen, sincerely. My head shrunk, when the spell faded, back in my open-topped crate. It just didn't shrink evenly. It became misshapen, would have been at home on the desk of Doctor Todd. Doctor Todd, and his misshapen skulls, believed in me, enough to send me to the archives, Clerk I, Special Opportunity Class. I didn't get off at the station by the hospital, where I ended up, after the incident at the archives, where I waited for Oksana. I went to the bar, black, pink, red. Alone, sat at the bar, on a red stool. It was earlier, the sun was coming in through the windows, opening onto the street. The red lights weren't strong enough, to paint the white pink. So it was, is black, white, red. I'm writing here, in this notebook, at the bar, in the bar. I'm not completely alone, there are others, under the red lights. Only, on the outside, the notebook is enough of a wall, between me and them. This isn't their made-up kingdom. I ordered a bourbon, Doctor Todd's whiskey. Doctor Todd was wrong, to send me to the archives. I mean, I didn't make it, ended back in the hospital, as a client. But he wasn't very wrong. Doctor Wimsatt, her bottle of gin, were right, but not very right. The same condition, the same title, working for the same government. As much ambiguity, uncertainty as the splattering of diagnoses of my father, over twenty years. I came here, to the bar, to capture the giraffes, elephants floating in the air, if they were still here. And they are still here. The giraffes were the same, Mfaume, Dot, Hi-Boy. Awkward, fragile, exotic, attracting record crowds, to the zoo. Those that made it, out of Africa, across the sea.

Elephants were different, so many more stories. They were there, at the zoo, from the very beginning. They were the beginning of the zoo, there was nothing but them at the start, marking its existence. Dunk and Gold-Dust, the names of the first two, both from the circus. What sticks, in my head, is cheap elephant material. Because there was cheap elephant material, though they didn't use the words, had nothing to do with cities, crocodiles, corruption. Mirga, the word used. Third-class elephant, in India. Legginess, lankiness, weediness. Fat trunk, thin back. Couldn't lift much, carry much. Not that steady, on its feet, in its eye, in its brain. Didn't matter much, in the zoo. An elephant's an elephant to most people. Very important, for the zoo, for collectors, out there buying them. Wouldn't do to pay first-class prices for cheap elephant material. With me, it was easy. Nothing that came out of the hospital, where I was a client, was better than third-class. It was what made Susan Buck so silly, in the end, after I had a chance, to think it through. She was selling me, to myself, as a Koomeriah, a first-class elephant. A broad-backed, barrel-chested, wide-trunked, bright-eyed specimen. Humans aren't put into classes, around here. I mean, they are, it just isn't really spoken about. Except when it is. Cheap human material, not acceptable. Clerk I, Special Opportunity Class, okay. The Board, Garbage Bin, were tried, convicted, killed, by a system that was supposed to treat people fairly, equally. Don't know if fairly, equally, meant the same thing, in the context. Regardless, the complexity of the system, the language, made it impossible. At least elephants, clients are classed for work, what they can do, not their meat, their religion, a hundred other things. Could always be worse, I guess. Images of Solomon Nagler's films appear now, whenever I think of Jews, World War 2. Even if what little I know about the war was learned at the hospital, where I was a client. Circus elephants tended to be Dwasala, second-class. They didn't need, didn't want to pay for, the best. But the animals still had to perform, in the ring, move cages, equipment, out of it. The reasonable middle ground, not exactly what circuses were known for.

I'm sitting at the bar, writing, with a whiskey, barely touched. Actually shouldn't drink, with the pills I take. Not recommended. In extreme moderation, doctors on the outside say, occasionally, when the subject comes up. If I must. They recognize the social side, of drinking. That for most of us, interacting is challenging. Avoiding parts of the ritual of interacting, makes it more so. They still can't recommend it. I always think, if I'm not mixing it with my daily coffee, I'll be okay. Not true, I know that, just what I tell myself. Don't really want to become Doctor Wimsatt, Doctor Todd. The first time I was here, in this bar, black, pink, red surrounded by the orange-brown haze, I spoke about giraffes, elephants for a reason. To avoid the subject of Oksana, her parents, to avoid talking about me. A distraction, personifying Jacquot, the generic parrot. If I'm being honest, with myself, this is just a repetition, in context. My aim is to be honest, with myself, writing, in this notebook, to work through things I have trouble understanding. Not playing, to what doctors, priests, want to hear. Not to make my life intelligible, general, dissolve my existence in the head, life of others. Yet I'm distracting myself, with elephant classes. Making loose analogies that never really hold together. My head's misshapen, askew for a reason. Many reasons, probably. I think it's because I should be angry, explosively furious. What Susan Buck said wasn't silly. It was manipulative. It was self-serving. It was horseshit. And, immediately, the next words, that want to come out, to be written, on the page. No blame, anger. No point. A part of my brain, bulging, trying to push through my skull. Another, calm, to the point of numbness, paralysis. Another flashes a warning. If I do anything, express rage, I'll be deemed a danger, to myself or others. Classed worthless human material, unfit for life on the outside. I'll be done, effectively dead, as I wait for death, behind the walls, of the hospital. Susan Buck will express warmth, sympathy, nobility to the world. In the story to be written, the painting to be painted, I would be the demon, tormented, tormenting. No grace, for me, not enough humanity for there to be anything left, after the sins are washed away. Maybe not sins, not sure if demons sin, exactly. Just sort of fits, with this section of the notebook, if I understand it correctly. No point is right, completely right. I'm not that different than The Board, Garbage Bin. I can't win, against those who can talk, communicate, interact. Those who learned what all those lines mean, in the gyms, because they grew up outside, in the world. Those without a family history, of mental illness, perversion. I'm not sure if Emma Hauck was conscious, of the days passing, writing sweetheart come, in the asylum. If she wasn't, I envy her. I really do. She just was, was her condition. Didn't have to spend every day managing it. Paranoid. I saw the incident, in the archives, coming, yet didn't see it coming. Was there and wasn't there. I'm supposed to be able to handle it. That's why I'm outside. And, of course, the next words, that want to come out, to be written, on the page. I'm good at managing my condition. My rage, the part of my brain boiling, is just a symptom, of my condition. Anything unreasonable, rash is a symptom. The nice thing about whiskey, is that it doesn't come with ice. By default, anyway. The glass in front of me, on the bar, doesn't have ice. I can write and the liquid doesn't change, just sits there, waiting for me, to take a sip. I never would have written that, the words above, if a doctor was going to read it. I know better, or think I do.

I can't relate to the quote Nurse Galverson wrote, at the start of the section. I'm writing my life, such as it is. Yet it's different. I found my own quote, reading Annie Ernaux's books, getting some context. Most of her books were written after a happening, the abortion, the death of one of her parents. She seemed to take the time, to reflect, to relate what happened as a story, a clear arc. One time, she just published her journal, as it was written, during a passionate adventure. Her words, emotions alternated between pleasure, anxiety. Anxious waiting, for unpredictable encounters, overwhelming pleasure, followed by more waiting. She wrote, in the midst of it, this doesn't make a story, just a tissue of egocentric suffering. That, I relate to, what I try to distract myself from. Ernaux's perspective was wonderful and impossible, for me. She had been married, had two kids, was a mother to them, had contributed to the world, through teaching, literature. She had met, exceeded what society expected of her. The rest of her life was hers, to take pleasure in, to suffer from. It was not open, to criticism, disapproval, judgment. To the end of my days, I will have to prove I belong, outside.

My brain goes back to elephants. It's the wise move. I've been stabbing the notebook, I think. The bartender's looking at me weirdly. They are floating, in the air, in the bar, black, white, red. The sun is fading, the white barely holds, ready to turn to pink under the red lights. I keep looking up, from the notebook, just to see the change. I don't really need to, the page I am writing on should turn, when the time comes. Babe, an elephant performing with the Ringling Brothers Circus, was almost refused, by the zoo. The zoo had become a place for circus animals, to live out the rest of their days, in peace. They had served society, performing, in a ring, travelling from place to place. But elephants went bad, became killers, of humans. When the call came, about Babe, the rejection was immediate. The zoo didn't need, couldn't handle, another bad elephant a circus wanted to offload. The circus was stunned, because it was Babe. Everyone knew Babe. Everyone loved Babe. She was not a bad elephant. It was all a misunderstanding. The zoo accepted her, in the end, and she passed the rest of her life there, with no obligation, to perform. The stories I recall, about bad elephants, weren't usually from zoos, never from the zoo. They seemed to be there, in the records, to show why, the zoo was so hesitant, to accept animals offered. Yet elephants were intelligent, adaptable, even as adults. One of the few animals bought, collected grown up. Adaptable up to a point, I guess. An African Elephant, at the Liverpool Zoological Gardens, went bad, was put down by a firing squad, thirty soldiers, two volleys. Mandarin, with Barnum and Bailey Circus, started killing people on a ship, crossing the sea. Not the first time, just the last. Hanged with a winch, cage thrown overboard. Topsy, at Coney Island, electrocuted, six thousand volts. Cyanide in bran mash was apparently common, though

I'm fairly sure there were no specific examples, in the records. So many reasons to be suspicious, even after thirty years, performing in the ring, pleasant enough. Until they weren't. I'm suspicious, of me, of my condition, what anger might trigger. I guess it's reasonable for others to be suspicious, too. Even if it isn't reasonable, it's what it is, the price to pay, to be outside.

Suspicion of the animal, the human-like. I'm writing, in a notebook, in a section titled Sins. They aren't my sins, I'm sure of it. And not only because I don't really understand them. They're the sins of the priest, from Marguerite Duras's article, the priest who killed two people, and wasn't put down. People were killed, for their crimes, back then. Just not him, people like him, whose existences completely dissolved in the head and the life of others. Annie Ernaux's abortion, illegal, bloody, difficult, absurd, was human, was the experience of Nurse Galverson, no matter how different the details may have been. The priest's killings, were human sin. He was tormented, perhaps by Susan Buck's sort of demons. He needed help, compassion, forgiveness. Articles were written, so many articles, newspapers sold. It was shocking, I guess, what he did, but there had to be something more. A connection, to others, readers, the jury. A connection that wasn't there, for The Board, Garbage Bin, with the two people they killed. Orphans, with a cardboard imitation understanding, of life, a photo-montage cut out from last year's mouldering newspapers. Not even any dark, unusual passions. A reckless hold-up gone bad, probably predictable, the result, had they thought it through. Which they hadn't, apparently. I wonder if it was the same, with the nuns. Centuries of abuse, not just because it went on behind walls, inside institutions, out of sight. The priests, others involved, were above suspicion, this sort of suspicion, though not above sin. And The Board, Garbage Bin, were suspected, treated with suspicion, well before they killed. It's just what it is. At least Babe the elephant's story ended well, a pleasant retirement, in the zoo, no more need, to perform.

After all that, writing, working through thoughts, feelings, I come back to not really being outside, not in all the ways that matter. Despite all the responsibility, the life skills, I was taught at the hospital, as a client, outside still meant freedom. I'm not beaver-like, okay either way, being at ease wherever. Being beyond the walls, the constant observation, of doctors. That was what my father longed for, in his plea. And I have been no different. I knew better, had experience, at the archives, elsewhere. I knew I was old, incapable of change. Yet I couldn't see it, not really. My condition has been calm, more or less easy to manage, since I left the hospital. It's probably only hysterical simulation, or simulated hysteria. I can never tell. Regardless, there will be no success, no story, no definite conclusion. It will always be there, the heart of my egotistical suffering. I can't change, but I can go home. To George, all the others. Sit down at the table, for dinner. Tonight's pierogi night. Not really interact, be welcome anyway. I can also try to move on, from what was set up, by the doctors, when I was sold to the world. Doctors get it wrong. Some of them had to be wrong, in their conclusions, about my father, over twenty years. Doctor Todd, his misshapen heads, weren't exactly right, with the archives. I don't think things are working, in my open-topped crate. It isn't sharp, hard concrete, but it isn't working. I've proven myself, I think. I mean, I'm still there, the magnetic name tags seem satisfied. I'm cheap human material, not worthless. Legginess, lankiness, weediness. Nothing like how Susan Buck described me. I'll probably end up in a crate anyway, but maybe there's a crate better suited out there, in which I can go nowhere in particular.

The page I'm writing these words on, is very pink now. There's whiskey left, it'll stay that way. Not as if finishing it would be part of some social ritual. Ordering the drink, paying for it are all that's required. If only leaving the misshapen skull behind was as easy. Time to get out of the city, back to the ring. Food is waiting.

It's a year later, I guess. Didn't date anything, still don't. It's interesting, looking back, how much bigger the sins section is, compared to sacrifices. Writing still, in a notebook. Moleskin, no weird sections, Catholic guilt I never really understood. Got in the habit of writing outside, not really outside exactly, just not in a writing room. Taking my notebook with me, a little portable room, where I can be alone, work through my thoughts, feelings. Just no longer with the extra walls I don't really need. Except when I do, but I mostly don't. Still taking Doctor Wimsatt's advice, about writing, to work through things. Just sent her a bottle of gin, Great Jumbina Gin, which is a thing now. One more liquid, at the Liquids Market. I thought I'd write a note here, in this notebook, to say that. The notebook Doctor Wimsatt read, told me to write in, about her bottle of gin. Gives a sense of conclusion, perhaps, even if nothing seems to reach a definitive conclusion. Oksana, Soupy, Ham is no more, as a being, singular. They never really were, I guess, except for me. I did get out, of my open-topped crate. It's made a difference, without making a difference. Still have to work, interact, even if only in a human-like way. Take the bus, head to an office, daily. It's good, though, the repetition, in context. Helps me manage my condition. The repetition isn't quite so repetitive though, working for Oksana, at Dot Distillery, in what's now the city. Jackboot became Jackalope, the second a silent more often than not. Oksana hums what condition my condition is in when she's around. It's all very wrong, the sort of wrong I remember writing about in these pages. Brothers Quay, the woman writing sweetheart come, endlessly. Isolated, in a room, with a grandfather clock. All very intense, the feeling of it all. It was wrong, the asylum, the experience of the inmate, yet the experience was captured, completely. Dot Distillery isn't an asylum, of course, real or imaginary. It's just that I've found something off, wrong, askew suits me. I've thought it through a bit, in the notebook, covered in moleskin. It's kind of the anti-Susan Buck. The anti-sacrifices/sins. It's the messiness, ambiguity Soupy liked to go on about. It's harder, to manage my condition, but that's okay. I'm good at managing my condition, my egotistical suffering.

The project went through, arrangements made. Some people adapted, especially the young ones. Some people didn't. I'm recognized, sometimes, in the street. People who talked to me, in the bunkers. They usually thank me, say I'm the only person they felt actually listened to them. Then they talk about their issues, now, related to the annexation, or not. And I listen. It helps fill my jack-o-lantern head. Don't generally remember them, though. There was just too many. The ring road's being built, as I write this. A solid, physical line at the edge of the city, which the city has already jumped. Creating a new ring, perhaps, for creatures, who can't survive inside. I'm not sure. I guess I'm no longer one of them. Anyway, Soupy, Doctor Soupy, finished his post-doc, found a job at a college, in a college town. Ham went the other way, to the metropolis. I imagine him filming crocodiles, corruption, though understand he's directing movies, shot with real cameras. And Oksana's still here, trying to balance liquids culture with the market, flitting around her distillery as a cockatoo might.

ABOUT THE AUTHOR

Trent Portigal is a writer of eclectic curiosities based in Edmonton, Canada. Previous books include Death Train of Provincetown *(2019),* The Amoeba-Ox Continuum *(2017) and* A Floating Phrase *(2016).*